"There is no friend as loyal as a book."
– Ernest Hemingway

The Liberation of
Mr. Delaney

Karen Sue Burns

This is a work of fiction. Names, characters, places, locations, and incidents are either products of the author's imagination or used fictitiously. Any resemblance to actual events, locales, or persons, living or dead, is entirely coincidental.

ISBN 978-0-9896027-1-6

Credits:

Editor — Vickie Taylor at
        CopyeditingSavesLives.com

Cover — The Killion Group

Dedication

As a reader I've probably read thousands of book dedications over the years. It's a much different thing to actually write one yourself for your own novel. With that in mind, I'd like to thank all the authors I've enjoyed reading for their wonderful stories and identifiable characters, and for the inspiration they've provided in writing my own plots and characters.

A special dedication goes to my first two grandchildren, Miller and Delaney. I'd also like to thank my family and friends who have encouraged and supported my writing efforts over the past few years. Y'all know who you are. This one's for you!

Chapter One

"Boo."

"Boo, yourself."

Hands on her hips, Zoe Miller surveyed the figure standing at the attic window. The dusty glass muted the outside light. He appeared almost normal. Yet, something about him seemed strange—his stance, casual yet alert, was more common to someone her own age than a decades-old ghost.

His black eyes boldly returned her look, and a bumpy chill crept along her arms.

"You finally caught me," he said.

"That's the way it looks to me." She lobbed a tight smile in his direction and then swung around to scope out the attic's cast-off junk. Battered boxes and ancient packing barrels were scattered over the scratched oak floor.

"You're not afraid?"

Zoe rolled her eyes. "Give me a break." She turned back to him. He stood next to an old rocking chair near the window. "Great, you're finally talking." She shrugged and spied the object of her search thrown in a corner. "Big deal. Why did it take you decades to get up the courage?"

"I have my reasons," he replied, one corner of his mouth hitching upwards. "Sure you're okay with me hanging around your house?"

"Oh, please," Zoe snapped. "You've been here so long you're almost part of the furniture. What can you do to me?"

"I might surprise you."

"Whatever!" The damned ghost had the nerve to wink at her before lowering himself to the chair and setting it in motion.

Zoe threw him a final squinty glance, shook her head, and grabbed a wicker basket off a pile of cardboard boxes. She slammed the door behind her and clomped down the narrow wooden stairs to the second-floor hallway. Why, after decades in the house, had the ghost decided to make his presence known? Even though he was irritating, his company in the attic wasn't frightening. Nana had told Zoe plenty of stories about the spirit who cried at midnight. How scary could a crying man-ghost be?

In the newly remodeled kitchen of her small but evolving house in the Montrose area of Houston, Zoe arranged three African violets in the basket. It was a belated birthday gift for Tina, her mother's twin sister and her favorite aunt. Zoe was late for their monthly gabfest lunch and turned to snatch a pair of scissors from a side drawer. Out of the corner of her eye she caught the outline of a body appearing across the kitchen. She grabbed the scissors, holding them poised for battle. Stepping backward and turning her head, she feared the worst. Her heart skidded to a stop. The spirit from the attic lounged casually against the refrigerator door.

"Damn it." Zoe waved the scissors at him. Her pulse kicked in while her irritation escalated. "Is it necessary for you to sneak up on me like that? Can't you announce your arrival with clanging chains or woo-hoo noises?" She didn't have time to deal with him right then. Aunt Tina would be on time and pacing in front of the restaurant.

"Sorry. I realized we hadn't been formally introduced." He underlined his message with a charming smile.

Zoe glared at him and snapped her fingers. "What's with you? I know you're the ghost who's lived in this house even before my grandparents bought it back in the forties. And, by the way, why can't we get rid of you? I remember Nana called you Charlie cause she didn't know your name." She used the edge of a scissor blade to curl the ribbon she had tied around the handle of the basket. "How come you're just now coming out of the closet?"

"Guess it felt right," he said. "Why aren't you afraid of me? Don't you find me scary?"

She stepped back from the basket and gave it a good once-over. It would please Aunt Tina. She then gave the ghost a full three seconds of ever-so-careful scrutiny.

He looked human. With longish blond hair combed straight back from his forehead, dark brown eyes, a clean-shaven jaw, and over six feet of a trim, athletic body, he could have passed for the man living next door. And he couldn't be much over thirty years old, in living years that is. His looks were pleasing to the female eye, including Zoe's. His clothes were on the antique side, though, brown knickers and a white pleated shirt.

"Seriously, you think you're scary?" She swallowed a giggle, doing her best to focus on something other than his sexy image. "I've heard about you my entire life. According to my grandmother, you've never once appeared ghostly except to float around a bit and snore at night. Big deal, dogs snore."

"Okay, okay." He raised his hands in mock surrender. "I admit it. I'm not the average spook in the attic. Of course, what is average today?" He chuckled to himself and raised worried eyes. "But still, we might as well try to get along since we both live here."

"No, I live here, and you, uh . . ." She couldn't produce the proper word to describe the living arrangement. It didn't matter that her grandmother had approved of him, doted on him even. Zoe would simply ignore him. "Okay, Charlie or whoever, I've put up with your noise for the past two months and—"

"Why are you living here?"

"I inherited the house from Nana. Anyway, it seems I can't get rid of you, at least for today. Keep yourself to the attic, and use a nose plug or something. I hate hearing a man snore."

"Oh." He raised his eyebrows. "You've had experience with men?"

"I'd love to share juicy slumber party stories with you, but I'm late." Zoe slung her purse over her shoulder and placed the basket in a shopping bag. She hurried to the front door.

He called out behind her. "My name is Ansel J.

Delaney III . . . in case you're interested."

After opening the door, she looked back at him. He stood in the doorway to the kitchen with light from the window illuminating his ghostly body. He was too attractive for his own good. Now, *that* was a scary thought. "I'd introduce myself as well, but I'm sure you already know my name." She winked at him and walked out of the house.

❧

As expected, her aunt waited for Zoe in front of the restaurant. A beauty of a woman, Tina simply didn't age. A flowing red, gold, and purple caftan concealed the slim figure she maintained by regular sessions with a personal trainer. Her expertly made-up face radiated warmth and a zeal for living.

"Darling, you've arrived." Aunt Tina embraced Zoe. After a moment she held her niece at arm's length. "Let me look at you. I don't see any dents or scratches."

It was an old joke between them—Aunt Tina would look over Zoe for signs of wear. Not once in almost thirty years had she ever expressed disappointment in Zoe, other than over one high school boyfriend whose gothic looks and inability to speak complete sentences aggravated everyone in the family.

"Auntie, I'm fine." Zoe took her aunt's hand and swung the shopping bag behind her back. "Let's get a table on the patio. This fall weather will be gone soon."

Once their lunch was ordered and two glasses of white wine served, Zoe dug in the shopping bag beneath the table and placed the basket of violets in front of her aunt. "Happy belated birthday. We missed you at Mom's party, but I know you were enjoying Honolulu."

"The violets are beautiful," Tina exclaimed. "Thank you so much. And yes, Hawaii was . . . well, let's say invigorating."

Zoe laughed, wondering just how invigorating the trip had been. "Good for you, Hot Mama Auntie." She sipped her wine and noticed Tina's quick display of dimples, which made her think of Ansel. "Guess who I talked to today? Think big."

"Hmm . . . the Easter bunny?"

"No, smarty-pants. I talked to our friendly run-of-the-mill ghost."

"Are you talking about the one in your attic?" Tina's eyes glittered with excitement. "I haven't thought about him since Mama died. She loved that ghost. She saw him only a few times, yet she loved the idea of sharing her house with a spirit."

"That sounds like Nana. She loved the unusual. He told me his name: Ansel J. Delaney III." The memory of his sexy look when she'd left the house sent a quiver along Zoe's spine.

"You've certainly learned more about him than Mama ever did. She tried everything imaginable to catch him off guard, but he was too quick." Tina raised a fist in the air. "Mama, Zoe has done it." She grinned and squeezed Zoe's hand. "She would be so proud of her granddaughter if she could see you today."

"I still miss her."

"I know you do, sweet pea. I have an idea." Tina's eyes flashed, a sure sign she had an interesting scheme in mind. "Why don't you do what Mama never could? Now that you know the spirit's name, find out who he is. What's his story? Why is he stuck in your attic? I bet if you did an Internet search on his name, you'd get a hit."

Zoe mulled over her aunt's suggestion, mentally tapping a pencil against the glass table. "I guess I could do some research. His story might make an interesting magazine article." She hadn't sold one in six months. The extra cash would bolster her fund to design a new backyard.

"Aren't ghosts supposed to pass to the other side?" Tina asked. "So when they're trapped in a building or in the middle, there must be a good reason for it." She leaned over the table and whispered, "A good reason like murder or a terrible accident."

"No way, that sounds too dramatic. Maybe he fell down the stairs or tripped on his shoelace. Who knows? I don't know anything about ghosts, so I'll check out the paranormal section at the bookstore." Tina's words had spawned a curiosity in Zoe about Ansel's life before his death. She muttered to herself, "I wonder why he's trapped in my attic." Perhaps it was payback for all of her days of mindless partying a few years ago. Her parents would probably tell her to accept her punishment.

"Sounds like you have a plan to me," Tina said. "By the way, you can check with the city about past owners of the house. You never know, one of them may have been involved in his death."

Zoe put a hand over her mouth to hide a giggle. Her aunt had read one too many mystery novels.

The luncheon salads were served, and the conversation turned to Tina's vacation in Honolulu and her handsome traveling companion. Zoe quickly concluded he was hot. Go Auntie!

~✧

Later that afternoon, Zoe had a hankering for her special marinara sauce. She pulled the ingredients from the pantry and refrigerator and set them on the brown-and-gold granite counter. After retrieving her cutting board, chef's knife, and stock pot, she pulled an oak stool next to the sink and automatically glanced out the window to the backyard. It wasn't much more than occasional tufts of grass sprinkled with Texas weeds.

She imagined its new design while chopping the onions. Bright red azaleas would march along the fence, and a flowing oak would shade the new brick patio. A noise behind her interrupted the landscaping daydream. She froze and set the knife on the cutting board. While holding her breath and bracing her hands on the edge of the counter, she slowly turned toward the noise.

Her breath rushed out, and she yelled. "Didn't we agree you wouldn't sneak up on me again? Remember? Clanging chains?" Although the ghost might be polite and cute, she surmised he had lost a good deal of brain function over the years.

"You're right. I'm sorry," Ansel said. He was now handsomely dressed in a yellow golf shirt and blue jeans. "Would it be more proper if I were to whistle to let you know I'm close?"

"Whatever, that's fine." Her breathing calmed. She finished the onions and began to mince the garlic cloves. "Why are you dressed different from this morning? Shouldn't you be wearing the clothes you died in and soaked in blood?" She peeked up from the cutting board. He now leaned against a counter three feet from her. Cool as a damned cucumber.

"I get tired of looking the same. Don't you?"

"Sure I do, but I'm a girl. How do you do it? Change clothes I mean."

"Magic." Ansel beamed and snapped the fingers of his right hand.

"That makes absolutely no sense." She placed the pot on the stove, drizzled in olive oil, turned on the burner. "Earth to Ansel, spooks aren't known for having designer wardrobes."

"Says who? Don't tell me you've read the latest edition of the spook rule book." He laughed, slapping his thigh.

"Very funny. Just my luck to live in a house with a dead guy who thinks he's a comedian." She stirred garlic and onions into the oil. "I can't believe I'm standing here having a conversation with you. This is too weird. How can you even talk?"

He shrugged his wide shoulders. "It's that old magic."

"That's ridiculous."

"Not if you believe in magic. And I do. It's what keeps me going." He looked at the floor, slowly shaking his head. "It's all I have."

"What the hell does that mean?" Zoe scoured his face for a hint of the man, or the ghost, behind his words. His expression remained the same—sadness mixed with resignation. She began to chop parsley.

"Are you trying to tell me something? Are you in this house for a particular reason?"

"There's a reason for everything." His mood shifted like the wind, based on the sparkle that had entered his dark eyes. "Didn't you learn that in high school science class?"

"That's silly." She stirred the pot with her favorite wooden spoon and faced him. "It's also insane that I'm having a semi-adult conversation in my kitchen, while chopping parsley, with a century-old glob of fog."

"Excuse me." He took a step toward her. "I'm not that old."

Zoe shooed him back with her free hand. "Mind your distance, mister. Don't forget, I'm experienced with a butcher knife."

"What a threat." He rocked back on the heels of his cowboy boots. "Let me rattle my chains in fear of your knife." A distant clanging of metal striking metal circled the kitchen.

"That's it. What a smart-ass you are. Go back to the attic," Zoe commanded, punching the air with her fist.

"Spoilsport, you need to develop a sense of humor." He then adopted a parental tone. "Seriously, I've noticed that over the past couple of months you've rarely laughed and seem down in the dumps most of the time."

She glared at him, itching to slap his face. "You must be the dumbest ghost in the state of Texas. I've politely asked you to go back to your roost in the attic. If you don't, I'll . . . I'll hire a ghost buster, and then you'll be history."

"Sweet thing, I'm already history. What's your excuse?" He disappeared with the faintest screech of a whistle filling the space he abandoned so quickly.

"Damn, damn, damn. I don't need this right now." Her fist pounded the counter. With everything undecided at the bookstore, this was not the time to deal with a slapstick spirit. The fact she could talk with him played as plain stupid and utterly ridiculous.

She finished mincing the parsley, and opened the tomatoes. Stirring all the ingredients together created a rich, dark red sauce and a delicious aroma.

Zoe declared to no one in particular that her simple marinara sauce smelled far superior to an old ghost with a smart-ass streak. But still, he had one hell of a butt. Although, was that a plus or a minus considering Ansel was dead?

Chapter Two

On Monday morning, in her cramped office in the back of Merlin's Favorite Bookstore, Zoe fired up a search engine on her computer. She'd realized the day before, while watching the Food Channel, she had failed to learn anything about Ansel other than his name. Frankly, his attitude had ticked her off. One more notch on her belt of irritating males, dead or alive.

She had sent him back to the attic without asking one serious question. Her upcoming thirtieth birthday was probably the cause of her recent depressed and short-tempered mood, which he had so aptly identified. How could he do that so easily? No doubt ghost magic or some psychic game he played. She typed his full name into Google.

The computer screen filled with website links. She selected one at random from the archives of the *Houston Chronicle*. A short news article dated June 14, 1938, popped up.

Local Business Leader Murdered

Ansel J. Delaney III, heir to the J&L Manufacturing fortune, was found murdered in the bedroom of a Montrose area home last evening. Found by his younger brother, Maxim, and his mother, Mrs. William. Whitmire, Mr. Delaney appeared to have been shot in the chest. Additional details were not available at press time.

"Since he's stuck there, he must have been killed in my house. That is too creepy," she said to the silent walls of her office. Which bedroom was the actual murder site? She prayed it wasn't the one she currently slept in. But what if it was? Would a gruesome event seventy years ago freak her out and force her out of her own home?

No.

Zoe had never been afraid of her own shadow, and she sure as hell wouldn't start now because decades ago someone had transitioned from businessman to wiseacre ghost in one of her bedrooms. She squared her shoulders and went back to checking the *Chronicle*'s other links. The obituary and a minuscule blurb six weeks after Ansel's death reported no leads had surfaced concerning the identity of the killer or the motivation for the homicide.

The lack of media attention for a prominent Houston resident was curious. His family must have had considerable influence with the local police back then. How else would the death of a well-known citizen not be sensationalized in the local press? That meant his family had lived in the area for several years and had built relationships in the community, or had money from the manufacturing fortune. Most likely it was both.

"Hey, Zoe, I made coffee. Would you like a cup?" Jill Dodd's head popped around the side of the striped curtain that functioned as an office door. She was a college student who worked part-time and provided a nonstop stream of celebrity gossip while immersed in stocking and straightening the store's many book stacks.

"I'll get some in a minute." Zoe rechecked the website links for another article—nothing of importance. The Delaney family must have been a major player in Houston seventy-plus years ago.

The need for caffeine prompted her to venture into the store. Sunlight streamed through the front windows, pooling on the oak floor by the "Witches Rule" display of children's Halloween books. The fragrance of French Roast spurred her on to the coffee bar. She filled her favorite red mug, took a sip, and enjoyed the first taste of coffee bliss—damn near perfection.

She later found Jill dusting and realigning books among the shelves.

"Jill, I need—"

Jill dropped a feather duster. "Geez, don't sneak up on me."

"Sorry. Don't concentrate so hard on dusting." Zoe picked up the duster and patted Jill's shoulder. "I know you love paranormal books, so I hope you can find a couple for me that focus on ghosts."

"Ghosts, huh?" Jill moved to the next row of bookcases with Zoe following. Jill ran her fingers over the top edges of books along a shelf, a six-inch row of rainbow-colored bracelets jingling on her arm. "Any particular focus?"

"Not really, just general information on spooks."

"Gotcha." Jill looked over the inventory and then pulled three books from the shelves and placed them in Zoe's arms. "These should keep you busy. Why are you interested in ghosts, by the way?"

"Don't you remember me telling you last year that my grandmother's house is haunted?"

Jill nodded, and Zoe continued. "I saw him the other day in the attic, and it got me wondering why he's there. I plan to write an article on why spirits never leave a building."

"Cool," Jill said, displaying a wide grin. "You saw a ghost, totally cool and awesome. Oh, I almost forgot. My brother is coming in this morning. He still wants to take you to lunch."

Was she ready to date again? Negative. "Jill, I don't think so."

"Are you sure? It's been six months since you broke up with Bill."

Zoe opened her mouth to reply, but Jill cut her off.

"I know, I know. You dated him for five years, and he got engaged behind your back. Does that mean all men are jerks? Of course not. Sam is a great guy, and he'd never—"

"Please." Zoe held up a hand. "I'm not ready to date." Although . . . she had met Sam several times, and he'd been a gentleman. And he had the bluest eyes with long dark lashes. It wouldn't kill her to eat lunch with an eligible thirty-something man. But, stop. No. She wasn't ready. The last thing she needed or wanted was to make nice-nice with a man. It would be a long,

long time before she could trust one after the disaster with Bill. Her heart was miles away from being whole.

"Thanks, anyway. Please give Sam my regrets. I'm going back to the office to work on the invoices. Add these books to my account."

An hour later, hunched over a battered and paper-littered desk, Zoe was in the zone, concentrating on a difficult customer account. She didn't hear the store's owner enter.

"Good morning, my dear."

Her hands jerked upward while her heart skipped a beat. Papers floated to the threadbare carpet. "Mr. Allen, good morning. You startled me. I didn't realize you were in the store." She hopped off the chair to gather the scattered invoices.

"My goodness, you're focused on your work. That's one reason I believe you'd be such a responsible owner of Merlin's." He took off his black cowboy hat and placed it on a spindle of the old coat rack in the corner. His bald head glistened, as did the Tony Lama boots on his feet. Although ready to retire and transfer his beloved bookstore to a new owner, he reinforced his ownership a few hours each week.

"Thanks, Mr. Allen. I haven't heard from your business broker in over week. Any news on the status of my offer?" She sat back at the desk to reorganize the invoices. She prayed her position managing Merlin's day-to-day operations would convince him she'd be a responsible owner. "Does he need more information?"

"No, no, I don't believe so." Mr. Allen patted her clammy hand. "You must be patient, my dear. These business dealings take time."

He left in search of coffee while Zoe's anxiety raced around the small office. When he patted her hand, she felt like his favorite pet or worse yet, his grandchild. Her shoulders slumped. Buying Merlin's meant everything. It meant showing her parents that her partying days were over. It meant proving to herself that she had a solid future as a business owner, one who could succeed on her own, without a man or a parent by her side.

By the end of the day, the invoices were recorded and mailed to Merlin's credit customers. It was a task that, thankfully, wouldn't need to be repeated for another month. Zoe locked up shortly after six o'clock and set the store's alarm system at the front door. She sighed as she fired up her compact sedan, thinking about her bid to purchase the store. Nothing was easy these days.

After a couple of long and difficult conversations with her father, a vice president at an oil company downtown, Zoe finally understood that acquiring a business, especially one that had been in existence for almost forty years, was not an overnight event. Regardless, her patience bubbled near the ready-to-explode level. Simply put, she wanted to know if she'd be the elated owner of the bookstore or be forced to change her career path once again. No way in hell would she go back to working at a bank. Talk about a boring job.

Once at home, she kicked off her shoes, poured a glass of merlot, and plopped into her favorite chair with the books from the store. Tasting the wine, she grabbed the first book. Apparently a spiteful ghost was the spirit of a person who had been murdered or harmed by friends or family members. It usually haunted the place where the death occurred or its burial site.

Hmm, was Ansel friendly or evil? Evil might describe him since he had been murdered, but that seemed improbable. Nana had never mentioned any events with him that bordered on weird or harmful. She could barely get a glimpse of him, even though she'd worked at it for years. It was headline news if he floated around the house or made scary noises at midnight.

He was one slick spirit, though. His recent habit of annoying Zoe might vaguely be termed as haunting. She tapped a finger on her lower lip, or it might be called being a pain in the ass.

She heard whistling, and there he was, across from her, reclining along the full length of the sofa with his arms folded behind his head. What a surprise.

She closed the book on her lap and scanned him from head to toe. Damn, he looked good horizontal. How could a dead guy be so attractive—eighth wonder of the world?

"I had a hunch you'd show up," she said.

"Your charm is too irresistible."

"Thanks." Zoe chewed on a smart retort for a nanosecond. Instead, she sipped the wine, rolling its flavor across her tongue.

"That's one of the things I miss the most." Ansel pointed to the wineglass on the side table. "What I'd give for one taste of a sweet little Bordeaux."

"You miss wine? That surprises me." The basics

of life were more critical to her than a glass of wine, even though she did enjoy a good cabernet. "What about breathing?" She managed to eliminate any sarcasm from her voice.

"My, my, you are one touchy woman." His magnetic grin soon faded. "However, you are one hundred percent correct. Breathing is critical. Wish I could." He rolled over on his side, a hand supporting his head. "But I do like your spunk."

"That's ridiculous," she sputtered. "You like my spunk." Men, even the dead ones, said the dumbest things. "What the hell does 'spunk' mean anyway?"

"You've got grit."

"I guess you're saying I'm not a pushover." He had that right.

"There you go," he said with a satisfying nod.

Zoe measured Ansel's words while stretching out her legs. "Thanks, I guess." His comment was a compliment of sorts, and for a mysterious reason, it melted one small cube of ice packed around her heart.

She shifted mental gears.

Would it be wise to explain the magazine article to him? If she didn't tell him, he'd never know and couldn't get angry. On the other hand, he might like the idea and offer real insight into the spirit world. Predicting his reaction was impossible since she had no clue to his personality, other than the smart-ass streak. No, that wasn't entirely true. Ansel did have a sense of humor, and every woman on the planet declared it the number one trait in a man. To enlist his help, she'd have to make it worthwhile.

"Ansel, I'd like to help you cross over to your

final resting place. But first, I need you to help me with something." She crossed her arms and focused all her energy on him. His eyes were a radiant blue rather the dark brown of the other day. They reminded her of the sparkling eyes of the baby dolls she had loved as a little girl. Asking him about his changing eye color was on the tip of her tongue, but she quickly changed her mind—better to keep the questions on target for the magazine article.

He laughed and sat up. "Let me make sure I have this right. You want to help me because I'm trapped in your house. To do that, I must help you first." His gaze bored into her eyes. "More details, please."

She stole a sip of wine, her mind racing like a greyhound at the dog track. She fingered the stem of her wineglass. "This is the deal. I want to redo my backyard, and to do that, I need money. One of the ways I make extra cash is writing and selling magazine articles. My plan is to develop one about you. I hoped you might help me with the research, and along the way we could figure out why you're stuck here and how to release—"

"Whoa there, hold on a damned minute." Ansel didn't miss a beat. He ran both hands through his hair while looking at the floor.

Zoe guessed he wasn't too happy with her.

He raised his head. His eyes were black and his face was blank. He crossed his arms over his broad chest and said, "I'm not sure about this, but . . . how may I help you? I imagine my aid with your article will in turn help me to escape the confines of this house."

Much relieved, Zoe licked her lips. He wasn't mad

at her after all, at least she hoped not. His face didn't match his words. "Yes, that's exactly what I was thinking. Your input will help me to create a terrific article. You could provide a perspective I'd never develop on my own, one with authenticity." She grinned. Her logic was superb. She crossed her fingers, hoping Ansel would accept her offer.

"Hmm, I see."

He walked to the front window and peeked out between the slats of the wooden blinds. She surveyed his strong back while wondering what he was thinking. The tucked-in white polo shirt outlined the distinct muscles of his shoulders and arms. She tilted her head, inspected the black jeans molded to his butt, and fanned her face with a hand. Goodness, he was one handsome ghost.

Abruptly, he turned around and faced her.

"This is what I'll agree to. I have limits. I can't give you information outright. All I can do is confirm or deny what you discover. That's the deal."

"That's ridiculous." Zoe rose and paced the living room. She stopped a foot in front him, and frustration settled into her words. "Are you saying you can't tell me this is the house you died in, or what bedroom, or why you died?"

"That's exactly what I'm saying." He moved toward the stairs, dismissing her.

"Stop right there. Why? Why won't you help me?"

Ansel turned to face her anger. "Zoe, it's not that I won't help you. The truth is . . . I can't help you."

She responded to Ansel's statement with pure

logic. "That's the dumbest thing I've ever heard."

He stared at her, scratched his nose, put his hands in the front pockets of his jeans. "I don't like this any better than you do. Jesus, will you have a little compassion for my situation here?" He stomped back to the sofa.

Zoe moved to the window, gaining distance from him. She looked through the blinds where moments before he had stood. She viewed the front yard. It was freshly mowed, and green and tidy. She turned back to her new buddy in the attic who sat on the arm of her green tweed sofa. "By the way, just what the hell is your situation that prevents you from helping me? It's not like I'm asking for your firstborn child or anything."

Ansel's usual flesh-and-blood manifestation faded. He became transparent, the normal appearance for a friendly, non-haunting type ghost. But from her viewpoint five feet away, he looked upset, unhappy, confused, or more likely, really pissed.

"What's wrong?" She froze at the thought of him being angry with her. She took a step backward, hitting a corner of the entertainment unit. What might an angry ghost do to her? "Why have you changed?"

"It's nothing I can talk to you about." He smiled through thin lips and then rose and stood stiffly before her. "Please don't be angry at me for saying so, but you have the compassion of a sea turtle." The smile morphed into an icy glare. "No, on second thought, you have one hundredth of the compassion of a sea urchin." The cascading racket of a train whistle filled the room from corner to corner. Ansel dissolved into a flash of iridescent blue fog. Within seconds the fog evaporated.

"Damn. What's his problem? That ghost has a lousy attitude. Go rock in your attic chair, you old rotting spirit." She clamped a hand over her mouth. That was a terrible thing to say about another person, ghost or not. She sat on the arm of the sofa. Being hardheaded was normal for her but being mean wasn't. Ansel had her going in circles. He continued to think like a man, and she'd had enough of men the last year, regardless of their state of being. She hoped that for once in her adult life, her days would move along the easy path. Although, with a ghost in the attic and her offer for Merlin's still up in the air, her probable route seemed closer to the 610 Loop during morning rush-hour traffic—stop and go with slow progress.

∿

Ansel paced the attic from the window to the door and back. The meager moonlight filtering through the window did little to brighten his mood. He couldn't think straight. He had no experience with a woman like Zoe, at least none that he could remember. Modern women were too complicated. They wanted to have it all, although he'd never understood what having it all meant. He shook his head. Recalling concrete details of his human life seemed impossible. Maybe he'd had it all when he was alive and didn't realize it.

He tried to understand modern life. When the house was empty, he watched all the talk shows on daytime television and kept up with current topics via cable news. But too many times he couldn't understand what they were discussing. Women talked too fast, and they didn't listen to one another.

He ran his hands through his hair and stared out the window. The street was empty of traffic. Today's cars zipped around at an amazing speed. He'd love to drive one. Like everything else he craved doing, driving a car was impossible due to the limits of his physical condition. Shouldn't he exercise the few powers he possessed and build on them? The *Ghost Rule Book* wasn't a joke, and he should take it seriously now that he had had a reason to use its teachings.

For instance, he could . . . well, damn it. He'd figure out how to be useful to Zoe.

His jaw clenched as he turned away from the dusty glass. The list of activities he couldn't do stretched from Houston to the moon and then to Mars. He chuckled at that. Now he was the one being dramatic, like Zoe.

He thought about their previous conversation, and his declaration that he couldn't outright help her with the details of his demise. The whole situation was unfair to Zoe. She didn't ask for any of this when she'd inherited her grandmother's house. He had been rude when she mentioned a firstborn child. She didn't know the true meaning behind her words. *Damn it, he would figure out how to help her.*

He rolled his long frame into the rocking chair, seeking relief from his worries, primarily Zoe. In fact, he felt sorry for her. The breakup with the boyfriend had been rough. He understood why women said men were dogs. He'd never have led a woman on like Bill had with her. A gentleman didn't do such things. Of course, he hadn't been perfect when he was alive. If he had been perfect, he wouldn't be stuck in the attic.

Zoe filled his mind. She was sassy and feisty and beautiful—long chestnut hair, blue eyes, a thin frame, and tall. He'd always liked tall women. A man didn't have to break his back to kiss one. They fit nicely in the circle of his arms, too. He could barely remember how it felt to hold a woman. Yet he'd never forget the comfort in his soul from holding another human so close.

He sighed, and the rocking chair began to move. Although she didn't realize it, Zoe had given him an opportunity, one that had been dormant for seventy years. He had no idea how to take advantage of the situation. His brain didn't work properly, but he would build on what he could, ghost magic included. He was patient, and time was on his side. He'd rest for a while and then mosey downstairs to check on her.

∾∾

Much later that evening, Zoe climbed into her wrought iron bed carrying a pad of yellow paper and her favorite green pen. The quiet before midnight was the perfect time to work on the magazine article. Her earlier annoyance with Ansel had evaporated, just like the blue fog.

The article would begin with a rundown of her topic followed by a point-by-point review of Ansel's "haunting" of her house. The conclusion, with him exiting her house, would be riveting—textbook feature writing.

She realized the conclusion created the most difficulty. She didn't have a clue to the ending, because obviously, the first act had yet to begin. Her earlier scuffle with Ansel was a sad commentary on her nasty attitude about her life in general. He had accurately assessed her mental state as being down in the dumps.

For the past six months she'd struggled to melt the emotional iceberg created by the unexpected end of her engagement to Bill, a man she had adored and completely trusted. Unfortunately, a magic potion to erase the memories eluded her, so the best she could do was one day at a time.

"My, my, you are a woman with a huge chunk of ice on your back. No, change that to choking off your heart."

Zoe's head jerked up. She frowned at Ansel, who lounged at the foot of her bed. "You were a psychiatrist before you kicked the bucket?"

"Must you be so nasty? That's rude."

"Rude? That's ridiculous." Zoe clicked her pen up and down. She couldn't believe the nerve he continued to display. "Being rude doesn't stop me from declaring you a pain in the butt."

"Sorry, you're right. I don't know what's wrong with me." He bowed his head.

She shot him a sour look followed by tears that slowly etched a path down her cheeks, dripping onto the yellow pad with a quiet splat. *Why am I being such a bitch? This behavior isn't like me.* She wiped her cheeks with her fingertips and folded her hands on the paper. Her brain was numb, and she felt like a moron for fighting with a ghost.

Ansel raised his head and observed her. She

wondered if he could hear her thoughts. For a dead guy, he possessed an uncanny ability to tune in to her moods.

Had his heart also been broken? Maybe that explained why he couldn't help her with the details for the article. He could have been killed by a jealous lover or by his lover's husband or boyfriend. Of course, that would mean he had no morals and was a womanizer, or not. No assumptions.

"I apologize. Since Bill and I broke up, I've been a terror." She fluffed a pillow behind her shoulders, aware of Ansel observing her every move. "I realize people break up all the time and it's not the end of the world. I need to put Bill behind me." He nodded, presumably in understanding, so she continued. "The life I had mapped out six months ago is gone. Living as a single person is what's best for me right now." She considered the words she had just spoken and grinned. "Yes, a new and improved attitude as a single woman is my new goal."

"I think that's admirable."

"I'll do my best."

"I apologize for my earlier comments. They were out of line." He sat facing her on the edge of the bed. "I'm one hundred percent positive we can reach an understanding about your article."

"Excellent." Another cube of ice dissolved, and the wings of Zoe's heart almost fluttered. "What's your plan?"

Chapter Three

Jill tugged a large cardboard box into the middle of the main walkway of Merlin's on Tuesday morning. Zoe opened it and pulled out a long string of orange lights. By midafternoon, she and Jill had finished setting out the annual Halloween displays. The store reflected the spirit of the holiday with ghosts guarding the aisles between the stacks, scary spiders and cobwebs covering the light fixtures, and a glittering garland of pumpkin lights over the store's entrance.

Standing near the front door, Zoe surveyed their work. "This looks fantastic. What costume are you wearing this year? I'm dressing as either a goblin or a go-go dancer."

"Haven't decided yet." Jill stood behind the checkout counter, cleaning its glass top. "I want something easier than last year's Goofy costume. It was too hot."

"Speaking of hot, I've changed my mind. I'd like to have lunch with your brother."

"Wonderful." Jill clapped her hands. "I'll talk to him tonight. Guess you decided it's time to move on, huh?"

"Something like that." As she walked to her

office, Zoe prayed an over eagerness to move on with her life hadn't persuaded her to agree to the lunch date. Only time would tell.

Her brain was frazzled after three hours of pinpoint concentration on an Easter inventory order. Even though she had worked in a bank for three years after college, she still detested working with numbers. It ranked right up there with cleaning a commode or dissecting a frog.

Somehow though, she'd have to get over her hang-up with balance sheets and profit/loss statements, as they were a staple in running a successful business. And, a successful Merlin's was her primary goal, in addition to preserving a good single female outlook. That reminded her she had two more days before calling Mr. Allen's business broker about the status of her offer for Merlin's. Fingers crossed.

To clear her head, she stood and performed a couple of jumping jacks followed by calf stretches. She wiggled her fingers, decided she needed a manicure, and sat back at the desk.

A fifteen minute break was in order. She clicked on the Internet search engine to check the local appraisal district website for pre-Nana owners of her house. Within seconds the property record appeared with two names—Charlotte J. Dodd and Ruth Everest Sims. The second name was Nana's, so the first person must have been the owner in 1938.

Maybe Charlotte Dodd was there when Ansel died, or maybe she was the killer. Zoe quickly dismissed that thought. She needed facts for her article, not her own tidbits of speculation. After all, she didn't know for certain that her home was the site of Ansel's murder. One more thing to add to her list of research topics, or perhaps she could finesse the information out of Ansel.

She glared at the Easter order lying on the desk. Her brain demanded a night off from worrying about the store and her offer to purchase it. She thought about the magazine article and muttered to no one in particular, "I know just where to go to get the facts. I'll talk to my favorite hunky spook."

∼✑

It had been a long and difficult day that now bordered on the absurd. Ansel was frustrated. The host of his favorite reality show was scheduled to appear on his favorite daytime cooking show, and then, the frosting on the cake, Bon Jovi was scheduled to sing on his favorite talk show. But could he get the television to turn on and then change the channel at his command? No, hell no. And recording the programs on the cable box DVR? Forget that. Everything, absolutely the entire macro level of his existence, was screwed up to the zillionth degree. At that particular moment, he was a mere skeleton of the ghost who regularly visited Zoe.

He settled into the attic rocking chair, his place of greatest comfort, and looked forward to the gentle motion calming his nerves. After twenty minutes, he rubbed his eyes with the palms of his hands and shouted to the ceiling, "Damn it. I hate this." Beating his fist on the arm of the chair or pounding a wall would provide no physical freedom. All he had to relieve his frustration were his mind and his voice—

neither capable of releasing the coiled tension driving through his empty gut.

The situation was ridiculous.

Stop. He sounded like Zoe again. How could he deal with the truth of their mutual predicament so both could win? He had to figure it out. Last night he'd told Zoe he planned to help her with her article. Had he developed the Plan? No. had he started to exercise? No. Had he tested his powers? No.

Doing nothing would stop now. Action, positive action that is, was his new motto.

The chair's motion slowed. It had been decades since he had seriously stoked his analytical brain. He figured it was similar to riding a bicycle: a person, dead or alive, never forgot how. The chair creaked as the speed of its action increased. Dormant synapses in his brain retrofired and began the long climb from the bottom of the well. They mouthed to one another, "It's about damn time." He privately prayed a guaranteed successful plan would eventually result from his efforts.

He heard a thud and a shout in the distance. The chair continued to rock and soothe until the hallway door to the attic stairs banged. Thumping moved up the stairs. Zoe soon emerged at the attic's entrance and zeroed in on the rocking spirit.

"Ansel, damn it, what the hell do you know about the smoke swirling from my cable box downstairs?"

He shrugged his shoulders and released the dead version of a calming breath. "Good evening, Zoe. How was your day? Mine was lousy, in case you might be interested."

She studied him. He maintained an innocent face under her scrutiny. After a moment she said, "We'll talk about your day later. Right now I want to know about the cable box. Any ideas on why it's not working?"

He shook his head.

She walked past him to the dirty window at the narrow end of the attic and peered outside. "Did you see a truck from the cable company on the street today?"

"Nope."

"Did you do anything worthwhile today?"

"Nope." He couldn't hold back and shot her a wicked grin.

"Fine. I'm going back downstairs."

Along with the surrounding neighborhood, he heard the rattling slam of the door and the stomp of Zoe's heels on the stairs all the way to the first floor.

Her improved attitude sure hadn't last long. She'd have to resolve that issue by herself. He had things to do.

The rocking chair creaked and once again embarked on its soothing journey. Ansel fought against a headache, the result of the unexpected brain activity. He had important work ahead—developing a strategy related to the curse placed on him. A delicate balance existed between his "living" arrangement and his new relationship with Zoe. His skills were frail at best, and he had severe misgivings about his ability to erase the curse placed on him. He hoped Zoe would soon learn of it through her own research for the magazine article. His very future depended on her success.

∼◡

Sam Dodd tackled the steps leading to his sister's apartment two at a time. Why the hell did she live in a building without an elevator? After three flights of stairs, his breathing barely hitched, and he knocked on the yellow door. It opened instantly.

"That was quick," he commented.

"I heard you stomping up the stairs."

"I don't stomp."

"Clomp, then."

"Uh-huh. You got any beer?" He was thirsty after all the climbing and followed her to the postage-stamp-sized kitchen. Jill handed him a beer. He popped it open, tossed down a satisfying swallow.

Jill moved away from him and sat at the computer table she had rigged in the corner of the living room. Sam remembered the day he had helped her lug the card table and metal chair from a thrift shop down the street. She had painted both a disgusting lime green. But she was proud of her efforts and credited her decor to the plight of the struggling college student. The rest of the room, with its sagging sofa, scratched coffee table, and cheap travel posters thumbtacked to the walls, completed the student-on-a-budget look.

The sofa sank under his weight, and Sam worked to stay upright. "Damn sofa. I wish you'd let me help you."

"Forget it. I've told you a million times I'm going to college on my own nickel, well, with loans anyway. I'm not using your handouts or drawing on the trust fund." She frowned before smiling. "You don't need to worry. I manage just fine. By the way, when is your lunch date with Zoe?"

"I figured tomorrow would be good. The due diligence for Merlin's is on Thursday. I need to question her before that. The attorney says she'll have to leave during our inspection since she's the other buyer. Doesn't she know every book in the store?" Sam remembered tales from Jill about Zoe's nearly faultless recall of the store's inventory. She not only remembered the title and author, but the publisher as well.

"Yep, her memory is incredible. Call her this evening to make sure she's available."

"Planned on it. I want her to think it's a date, not an inquisition." He finished the beer and struggled up from the sofa. "What's her home number?" He tossed the empty can into a wastebasket with a happy face on the side.

"I've already written it down for you." Jill handled him a pink Post-it Note. "She's not going to be happy when she finds out there's another buyer for Merlin's."

"I realize that. But posing as a buyer is the only way for us to search the store without her around. Unless we break in—"

"Break in? No way."

"Don't worry, that's a last resort." Sam kissed his sister on the cheek and headed for the front door. "Remember to keep your eyes open."

"I know, I know," Jill waved a hand at him. "*The Adventures of Tom Sawyer* is permanently etched on my brain."

"Good. I'll call Zoe to arrange that date."

~~

Zoe smelled the yellow roses she'd picked up at the market on the way home from work. They were a bit of a splurge and worth every penny. She arranged the blooms in Nana's favorite cut-glass vase and filled it with water. The last time she had bought flowers for herself was six months ago, after the last date with Bill. Back then, it was to cheer her spirits. She'd been blindsided by the end of their engagement and transitioned into a mini tailspin. Thankfully, it hadn't lasted for more than a few weeks. Today, the flowers marked another transition.

Her declaration to Ansel the other night had troubled her the past two days. For her own peace of mind, she needed to get on with her life. She smelled the roses one last time and set the vase in the middle of the kitchen table. Bill was in the past. He would remain there, in both her heart and her mind. She wouldn't describe herself as truly happy, but she teetered on the edge of happiness, imagining new adventures and eventually, romance.

After her lunch with Sam Dodd, she believed a new man might be on the horizon.

They met at the Backdoor Café, one of her favorite bistros in the museum district of Houston. Sam had been a gentleman, as well as charming, a witty conversationalist, and drop-dead gorgeous. Sitting across from him gave her a perspective she'd never imagined from the casual encounters when he'd visit Merlin's to see Jill. She had no idea he'd turn out to be a twelve on the ten point hunk-o-meter.

Over shrimp cocktail, he relayed a story about his college days and one football Saturday at Texas A&M

when his fraternity had sponsored twenty children from a local adoption center. It was a pleasant surprise, as she had expected a story about frat house punch brewed in garbage cans and wet T-shirt contests.

They even had a conversation about their favorite wines.

"I'm a reds girl: merlot, cabernet, pinot noir, Chianti," Zoe explained, thoroughly enjoying the conversation. "Whatever fits my mood and goes with a good marinara sauce."

"I agree. Although I do enjoy a good chardonnay every once in a while," Sam replied. "Tell me your favorite foods."

"Sure, any recipe that's Italian, Mexican, French, Greek, or good old Southern home cooking.

One thing had led to another, and by the end of the lunch, Zoe had invited him to dinner on Friday evening. He volunteered to bring the wine since she'd be cooking. She later wondered why she had invited him to her home when she barely knew him. But then again, he was such a decent person and so easy on the eyes. It would be fun to cook for a man again. She smiled in anticipation. The redesign of her life was rolling right along.

Later that evening, Zoe stared at her computer monitor in the study. Her intent had been to devote a couple of hours toward the magazine article, but she was having a tough time getting her head around the opening paragraph. Sam's sky-blue eyes and dark lashes distracted her from the perfect first sentence. He'd been such a surprise. To think she had turned him down so many times during the past several months—

ridiculous on her part.

She gave herself a mental shakedown and typed the title: "Spirits Who Overstay Their Welcome." She began the introduction:

Ghosts and goblins are expected visitors on Halloween. But what does one do with a ghost who hangs around 365 days a year? One who simply won't leave, ghost busters or not. One who is ridiculously annoying and routinely scares the family dog. One who is lazy and loves to rattle chains and emit nasty aromas throughout the house.

What would you do? This is the story of what I did to erase the nuisance of a spirit from my attic.

While rereading the opening, Zoe heard whistling and swiveled in her chair. Ansel relaxed against the frame of the study's door. He wore a black T-shirt, jeans, and an infectious smile.

"You working?"

"I began the magazine article." She noticed his forearms, thick and strong. "Distracted, though."

"What's going on?"

Zoe figured he'd be uncomfortable with her since she hadn't seen or spoken to him after stomping out of the attic.

"Sorry about my bad mood last night," she said. "I'm frustrated about my offer for Merlin's. Waiting is the pits. I just want to know."

"I know what you mean about waiting. I hate it."

She gave him a sharp look. What was he waiting for?—a house fire or a bomb so he'd be forced to go somewhere else? Or was there something else?

"Don't you like the attic? Is there a problem?" She searched his face for a clue.

"Just because I'm stuck in the attic for eternity, why should there be a problem?" He said in a husky voice.

"Okay, okay. I get your point. Your life, uh, existence sucks." She searched his face again for a glimmer of self-pity. There was none. He simply watched her. She turned back to her computer. "Change of subject. Listen to the opening of my article." While reading it, she sensed his presence behind her. A breath of cool air fluttered across the back of her neck. She shivered.

"How does that sound?" she asked.

"Is it for a humor magazine?"

"Absolutely not." Zoe was surprised he'd ask such a silly question. "Why would you think that?"

"No reason. I guess I haven't kept up with modern journalism."

"Apparently not. This is a simple feature article with maybe . . . perhaps, possibly a small touch of humor. Nothing major. Understand now?"

"Uh-huh, sure." Ansel leaned over her shoulder while gazing at the computer screen. "The print is small. How can you read this?"

He moved closer to the screen, and the front of his chest passed through Zoe. She jumped, startled by an electrifying sensation that began in her left shoulder. It leaped to her chest and traveled straight down the center of her body before exploding into a stream of sparks throughout her abdomen.

He must have sensed it too, as he quickly moved back to the doorway.

She caught her breath and searched his face for an explanation. It was blank.

After a moment he smiled. "How was your day?"

He did feel something, like a spark or a firecracker when he touched her back. And now he doesn't want to talk about it. *How typically male.*

"It was good. I had lunch with a guy who may have potential."

He raised an eyebrow. "Really?"

"Yep, I'm on the road to my new life. It feels great. He's a cutie, too."

"A cutie? What's that?"

"You know, an attractive man. I have a good feeling about him. He's a great guy."

"Good for you," Ansel snapped. Then he was gone, evaporated into clear air, no blue smoke.

"What's his problem?" Zoe muttered, throwing her arms up in the air. Within five seconds she heard the familiar sound of chains clanging in the attic, followed by the ringing of a phone.

She picked it up in her bedroom.

"Zoe, I must speak with you."

"Mr. Allen, what's up?"

"I don't want you to be upset by this, but I've received another offer to purchase Merlin's."

"Oh, no." Zoe nearly dropped the phone. Why would he consider another offer?

"Now, my dear, this is the way business goes. We do have another legitimate proposal. I can't ignore it. The due diligence is scheduled for tomorrow afternoon."

"What? Tomorrow afternoon?"

"That's right. Since you're also a potential buyer, you'll need to take the afternoon off, paid of course."

Her stomach twisted into a knot. Good lord, another buyer? Could her life get any worse? She had no choice but to agree with Mr. Allen.

"If that's what you want me to do."

"Glad you're on board, my dear."

Zoe clicked off the phone and wondered who the hell was screwing up her plans to own Merlin's. She stamped her foot like a three-year-old. Damn, this sucked.

Chapter Four

Zoe tossed and turned during the night and reluctantly dragged herself out of bed Thursday morning. She had been hot, then cold, all the while remembering Mr. Allen's phone call. Losing Merlin's would be tantamount to losing a best friend. She couldn't imagine working anywhere else. The book business was in her blood. It had grown on her, and she refused to sever the bond. Her eyes welled up. She brushed the tears away and reminded herself it wasn't over. A final decision had yet to be made, at least she hoped so.

A hot shower improved her maudlin mood and warmed her stiff muscles. She threw on her favorite yellow bathrobe and began her morning ritual of makeup and hair. She applied mascara to her lashes and inspected her hair. The blonde highlights designed to brighten her brown locks were in need of a touch-up. She could probably use a trim, too. She pulled the whole mess back into a ponytail.

"Why do you put all that stuff on your face?"

She gritted her teeth and turned away from the sink. "Stop sneaking up on me. Whistling, remember?"

Ansel grinned, settled on the cover of the

commode. "Sorry. But why do you it? Your face looks fine to me being plain."

"Plain?" She looked at her image in the mirror. She had always thought mascara enhanced her eyes. "Get serious. You don't understand the complexities of the modern woman. We simply like to look our best." She smiled at herself and applied a dusting of powder to her cheeks and nose.

"I didn't mean plain as in plain looking. You have natural beauty."

"Thanks." The comment pleased her. "If you expect me to talk with you, I need coffee. I'll meet you in the kitchen." She turned back to the mirror and dabbed on lip gloss.

Besides a nice glass of merlot, strong coffee was one of Zoe's preferred pleasures. She rotated three pots depending on her mood. This morning she had used a two-cup drip pot and Sumatra dark roast coffee.

"Mmm, I love strong coffee," she remarked to Ansel, who sat on the kitchen stool.

"Me, too." He watched her pour a cup like a dog watching a steak on a barbeque grill. "I miss it almost as much as a glass of wine. Funny how the simple things are what you miss when everything is gone."

"Guess that tells us the basics in life, like family and friends, are what's important."

"Especially, when you have nothing." He threw her a pathetic look.

"Sorry, guess you're the exception." She smiled and sipped the coffee. She watched Ansel out of the corner of her eye. "But you do have me, so don't feel you're alone. I'll be your family for now. We'll figure out your problem, and then you'll be on your way to . . . to your final resting place."

She hadn't given any thought to a future without Ansel in her house. Sure, he irritated her, and he seemed touchy, which was understandable given his status as a ghost. She might even miss him. Having him around was fun, like having a roommate without all the usual drama.

"My final resting place, that sounds ugly." He grimaced.

"I could check it out for you. See what the headstone is like or if the setting is pretty." She warmed up to the idea. This would be a meaningful way to help him. "I'll even take pictures for you."

Ansel didn't appear as enthusiastic as Zoe.

"Sure, that would be nice."

She glanced at her watch. "Gotta go or I'll be late. Have a good day."

"You as well, my love," Ansel replied as the front door closed.

❧

A regular Thursday event at Merlin's was a ten percent discount on any item for customers with a preferred buyer's card. The card had been Zoe's idea a year ago after some fast-talking to convince Mr. Allen. It had proven to be a resounding success, and this Thursday was busy, as usual. It was almost eleven before she had a chance to call Aunt Tina.

"Hey, sweet pea, what's up?"

"I have the afternoon off. Another buyer is coming in to inspect the store, and I can't be here. Would you have time to go with me to the downtown library?"

Zoe kept her fingers crossed. She didn't want to do this alone. "I want to visit the genealogy archives."

"I'd love to. I'm taking a break today."

"Excellent. I'll pick you up around one o'clock." Zoe was elated to have her aunt as her research buddy.

"By the way, an old friend of mine is the director there. I'm sure he'll be a good resource if he's available." She heard anticipation in her aunt's voice. Huh?

By twelve thirty, Zoe jumped in her car and headed to her aunt's house. The potential buyers were to arrive in thirty minutes, so she made sure she'd be far away from Merlin's when they arrived. Aunt Tina lived in the west university section of Houston on a beautiful tree-filled lot. Zoe always thought of the house as magical with its many wind chimes and colorful yard sculptures. Her aunt sat on the porch, lazily rocking back and forth on an outdoor swing.

Within minutes they were dodging an assortment of vehicles driving toward downtown Houston.

"Tell me about this other buyer," Aunt Tina said.

"I don't know much. Mr. Allen called last night."

"Couldn't he have told you earlier?"

"I don't know why he didn't. They're taking the afternoon to give the store the once-over with their attorney. That's why I had to leave."

"I'm sorry, sweetie," Tina said, sympathy coloring her words. "But let's be positive. Things will turn out the way they should."

"Let's hope that means I'm the owner of Merlin's," Zoe said and realized she truly had no other choice.

The main branch of the Houston Public Library was on the corner of Lamar and Louisiana streets. Zoe parked in the underground garage, and they rode the elevator to the third floor of the library.

A woman who reminded Zoe of Bilbo Baggins from *The Hobbit*, one of her favorite books, manned the information desk.

Aunt Tina obviously missed the likeness or hadn't read the book. "Good afternoon. We're here to see Theodore Ward."

The Bilbo look-alike nodded and picked up a desk phone. Within thirty seconds they were greeted by a distinguished-looking man—gray hair at the temples, tall with a good build, and laughing brown eyes. His eyes immediately focused on Aunt Tina.

"Tina, what a pleasure." He captured both of her hands in his own and brought them to his lips for a lingering kiss. "It's been much too long since I've seen you."

"Teddy, I agree, it's been much too long." She smiled and damn near swooned in front of him.

Zoe watched the two of them in awe. She had never seen her aunt flitter about in the presence of a man, any man, not even her husband, who had died years ago. This Teddy person was a different flavor.

Teddy and Aunt Tina were holding hands, grinning, and gazing at each other, seemingly oblivious to their surroundings.

"Mr. Ward, I'm Zoe Miller, Tina's niece."

Their connection broke, and the two turned toward Zoe.

"I'm sorry sweetie, what did you say?"

"I just wanted to introduce myself to Mr. Ward." Zoe looked from one to the other and made a quick decision. "I think it would be more efficient if we split up for the research. I'll take two names and you take the other two." She handed a piece of paper to her aunt. "I'll be over at the public computers. Okay?"

Tina glanced at Teddy and then at the paper. "We'll discover all we can about Maxim Delaney and his mother, Mrs. William Whitmire."

Teddy shook Zoe's hand. "It's a pleasure to meet you. I'll help Tina with her research. If you need any help at all, simply talk to Mrs. Bagby at the information desk." He pointed to a group of cubicles off to his left. "The computers are housed over there."

"Thanks. We've got a plan. Aunt Tina, meet you back here in about two hours. Okay?"

"Absolutely." Aunt Tina and Teddy headed in the opposite direction of the computer cubicles. Tina called out over her shoulder, "Have fun, Zoe, dear."

Damn it. Zoe should have been at Merlin's planning the Christmas displays. Instead, she was at the library wasting time since the research could easily be done at home. And Aunt Tina was off canoodling with a good-looking man.

Zoe stalked to the cubicles. Most were empty so she selected one at the end of the second row. After a couple clicks of the mouse, she forgot her annoyance and became engrossed in gathering the fragments of information available on Charlotte J. Dodd. The amount of research data available online was amazing. It was like having a full set of encyclopedias at her fingertips.

Almost two hours later, Zoe notated a final snippet on the Dodd family tree and felt the feathery touch of something running across her shoulders. She jumped out of the chair and knocked into Aunt Tina.

"Are you trying to scare me to death?"

"Sorry. Living with a ghost sure has made you jumpy." Aunt Tina chuckled, steadying her niece with a firm hand. "Are you finished?"

"I'm not jumpy," Zoe insisted. "And yes, I'm done. What about you and Mr. Handsome?"

Aunt Tina blushed. Zoe had never seen her aunt react so girly about a man.

"Teddy and I found some intriguing facts. He's just finishing up for you. We were hoping you might join us for a glass of wine at the Hyatt." She leaned toward Zoe and whispered, "I think he found something he wants to discuss with you in person."

"Okay. We can meet him there."

"I'll let him know we're on our way." Tina disappeared around the corner of the cubicle.

"This should be good," Zoe muttered as she stuffed pages of notes into her purse.

∽

The lobby bar of the Hyatt Regency Hotel used to be one of Zoe's favorite happy hour spots, as Bill worked nearby. Her heart experienced a momentary pause as she crossed the marble lobby, but then resumed its normal steady beat as she dumped thoughts of Bill permanently from her mind. He was so in the past.

She followed her aunt to a booth opposite the long oak bar. The subdued lighting created an intimate setting. Zoe figured she was good for one glass of wine. No doubt Teddy would offer to take them to dinner, Aunt Tina would agree to the wonderful idea, and Teddy would offer to take Tina home once Zoe declined the invitation.

Teddy appeared after their wine order was placed. The waitress glided back to the booth.

"Hi, Mr. Ward, the usual?"

"Yes, Amanda, that will be fine."

The drinks arrived, and their polite bar chatter stopped. Aunt Tina patted Teddy's hand.

"Teddy, please tell Zoe what we discovered about Mrs. Whitmire." She fixed her gaze on Zoe. "This is most unusual."

Zoe perked up. "I'm all ears."

Teddy began. "As you may know, the Clayton Library holds private collections from many of Houston's historically prominent families."

Zoe nodded. "I looked at an online book detailing the Delaney family history."

"What I'm going to tell you isn't available to the public, at the family's request." Teddy sipped his drink, drawing out the suspense. "Mrs. William Whitmire, formerly Mrs. Ansel P. Delaney, lived to the ripe old age of 104. Further, she died on the fiftieth anniversary of her son's death, June 14, 1988."

"You mean Ansel, right?" Zoe asked.

"Yes, Ansel," Teddy replied. "Now, that's curious enough in itself. There's something else that's even stranger."

"That's some coincidence about the date of death." Zoe's mind ricocheted from a mafia hit on

Ansel to his mother knowing the name of the murderer. "What else is strange?"

"It appears that Mrs. Whitmire kept a diary, a personal journal, for fifty years, from age twenty-five to seventy-five." Teddy's eyes twinkled.

"Okay." Zoe looked first at Teddy then focused on Aunt Tina. "How does her journal relate to Ansel? Was he mentioned in it?"

"Yes, sweetie, he was mentioned," Tina replied. "Quite a bit, in fact." She studied her niece for a moment as if weighing her next words and continued. "Zoe, we think the gist of what relates to your situation is that a curse was placed on Ansel and—"

"A curse! You've got to be kidding." Zoe paused and thought for a moment. "Is that why he's stuck in my attic?"

Teddy glanced at Tina. A silent message passed between them. Zoe wondered about their history. Whatever, this curse held more interest for her.

"What kind of curse? How in the hell could a ghost have a curse?" Zoe ran two shaky hands through her hair and leaned over the table, gazing directly at Teddy. "Who would be crazy enough to place a curse on a dead person?"

"Let me give you the ten-cent story." Teddy cleared his throat.

"Fire away," Zoe said as she leaned against the back of the leather booth, anticipating a doozy of a story.

"It appears Mrs. Whitmire started her diary when she was twenty-five and Ansel was three. Her husband, Ansel's father, gave her the first diary for her birthday.

She was consistent in her day-to-day entries. Her chronology of their family history points to a couple of interesting facts." Teddy paused and sipped his scotch.

Zoe paused as well. She hoped, no, prayed that Teddy and Aunt Tina had discovered the key to releasing Ansel from his intermediary post in her attic. He deserved that.

Teddy continued. "The first fact we discovered isn't so unusual. Mrs. Whitmire was devoted to her firstborn child. In fact, her devotion bordered on an obsession. She was overly involved in Ansel's life, even after he became an adult."

"Now, Teddy, that is subjective," Aunt Tina interjected. "I don't have any children, but if I did, I'm sure I would have been called a buttinski more than once."

Teddy kissed Aunt Tina on the cheek, and Zoe's jaw dropped. What the hell was going on?

"You would have been a wonderful mother, Tina. On the other hand, Mrs. Whitmire appears to be the extreme example of a caring mother, which leads to the second interesting fact. As Tina said before, her diaries indicate she put a curse on her favorite son shortly after he died."

"You're joking." Zoe nibbled on her lower lip. She found it impossible to believe a mother would place a curse on her own child—to force him to live, to exist as an apparition in house that wasn't even his. That was plain cruel. "This is too weird. Poor Ansel."

Tina gave her a sympathetic look. "No, sweetie, we're not kidding. It's all in her diaries. I've no doubt the woman was mentally off.

~✍

Zoe left Aunt Tina and Teddy at the bar just as she'd predicted. Damn she was good. She exited the library garage and headed home.

The car's digital clock read 5:35 p.m., so the due diligence at Merlin's should be over. Surely the other party didn't have the same desire to buy the bookstore as Zoe. No way. Merlin's was rightfully her gig and no one else's. If only there was something she could do to convince Mr. Allen she was the right buyer. Her better judgment told her to be patient and pray. Damn it. She didn't want to be patient, and she didn't want to pray. She wanted to own Merlin's.

She arrived home enveloped in a cloak of fake patience and looked forward to a relaxing evening. She planned to mull over the new information about Ansel and his mother and to work on the magazine article. However, a relaxing evening wasn't in the cards.

It began simply enough.

She changed into sweats and headed for her favorite room in the house, the kitchen. After pouring a glass of merlot, she tossed a green salad for dinner. With the pile of notes from the library, she sat at the wrought iron bistro table. Written in Italian across a corner of the sage green wall were the words for "Enjoy good wine, good health, and a long life." She'd own that motto once she purchased Merlin's.

As she munched, Zoe tried to gather her thoughts into a coherent list for the article, but she kept mixing them with Ansel's curse. Writing them on paper would help her stay organized. She drew a line on a blank a piece of paper from top to bottom, then labeled the left side "Ansel" and the right side "Magazine Article."

She heard a faint train whistle and sensed Ansel's presence in the kitchen. She looked up, and he sat across the table from her, grinning.

"Good evening, Zoe. Did you have a pleasant day?"

"Your timing is perfect." Her heart took an unexpected lurch at the sight of him. Where did that come from? Oh, no, surely she wasn't getting too attached to him.

"One of my many talents." He shot her a wicked grin. "Tell me how your day went. *I am interested.*"

"My day was both good and bad."

He raised his eyebrows.

"Okay. The bad part was that I had to leave Merlin's in the afternoon. Someone else has made an offer to buy the bookstore, and their official once-over of store operations was this afternoon. Naturally, I couldn't be present."

"I'm sorry to hear that. Who's the other buyer?"

"I don't know." Zoe sipped the wine and ignored her fascination with the fact she was sitting in her very own kitchen talking to a hunky dead man. "Anyway, I left the store, and Aunt Tina and I went to the Houston Public Library for research on—"

"Research?"

"Ansel, please," Zoe said slowly. "Do you or do you not want to hear about my afternoon?"

"I do."

"Let me finish." Zoe stabbed at her salad, once again trying to gather her thoughts into some semblance of order. What was that old saying? An orderly mind is a practical mind. She sure hoped so.

"The most interesting tidbit we discovered was that your mother put a curse on you and—"

He jumped from the table and backed across the kitchen to the sink. "How did you find out?"

"Aunt Tina and the library director found it in the family history section."

He rubbed his face. "I had no idea anyone else knew."

"Your mother kept a diary for fifty years. That's where they found it. Apparently you weren't the only one who received a curse."

He stared at her, disbelief written on his face. "I don't believe it."

"There were several mentions of her dissatisfaction with the gardening staff. Something about a spell to—"

"Stop." He raised a hand in front of his chest. "I don't want to hear it."

Zoe closed her mouth while Ansel turned toward the sink. Arms across his chest, he stared out the window at the backyard. Several minutes passed while a cloud of silence settled over the kitchen. She'd give him time. She jotted notes on the paper, thinking of the best way to approach him for details of the curse. Earlier he'd said he couldn't help her, but surely that didn't relate to a curse.

She heard a whistle and glanced up from her notes. Ansel once again sat across from her. He pushed his hair back from his forehead, rested his elbows on the table.

"We earlier discussed what I can and cannot say.

Do you remember that conversation?"

"Yes."

"Then you'll recall I said I can't help with your research for the article. At least anything specifically related to me."

"Fine, whatever," Zoe said. Talk about beating a dead horse. No problem. She could handle the research without his help. "I've got it covered." She carried her dishes to the sink, poured another glass of wine.

"What wine is that?" Ansel asked, changing the direction of their conversation.

"Merlot. I'm a fan of dry reds." Zoe swirled the deep red liquid in her glass, returned to the table. "Have you ever tasted this variety?"

"No. I don't recall that grape. It must be new."

"Not really, but compared to 1938 I guess it is a new wine." Poor Ansel, he had missed so much joy of life by dying young. A notion popped into her head.

"I won't ask you about the curse. I'll figure that out on my own. I have an idea. What if I helped you taste my wine?"

"Oh-kay. How?"

"I'm thinking." Zoe placed an index finger on either side of her temples, concentrating on how a spirit could drink wine. "I have a plan."

"That was fast. What is it?"

"Follow me." Carrying the wineglass, she moved into the living room, settling on the sofa. Ansel followed and rested a cushion away from her. She scooted toward the middle. He stared straight ahead.

"Don't think or question me," Zoe directed. "Go with the flow here."

"The flow?"

"Pay attention." Zoe reposed thigh to thigh alongside Ansel. "My guess is we need to concentrate hard to make this work. And, uh, maintain positive energy." She ignored his chuckle and sipped the merlot. "Taste me."

He gawked at her. "Are you out of your mind?"

"Now! Do it now."

He hesitated, leaned toward her. She readied herself for the electrical charge. His body pressed to hers, their lips lightly touching. Nothing, not even a fizzle. Yet, for one sweet moment, his lips reminded her of fresh fallen snow, soft and gentle and comforting. With increased pressure from Zoe, something changed. His mouth opened and she tasted his breath—a taste that ignited, deep in her center. It was too much. She pulled back.

"I can't believe it. I could feel your lips." She touched her own in disbelief. She looked at Ansel with narrowed eyes. "Are you a witch, or, uh, a warlock?"

Masculine laughter circled the living room.

"Good heavens, no. What an imagination you have," he said. "Maybe you should cut back on the wine."

"Whatever," she snapped. "You explain why I can feel your touch when you're supposed to be a spirit, not flesh and blood with a physical body. Tell me what's going on if you're not a witch."

"I'm not a witch, and you didn't feel me touch you." His voice had softened.

"I know what I felt," Zoe reminded him.

"You didn't physically feel my lips. It was a

mental sensation. Your brain told you."

"Huh?" She squinted at him. "You're sure about this?"

"I'll prove it to you." He scooted closer to her. "Now, keep that positive energy flowing. Concentrate."

Ansel placed his hands on Zoe's shoulders and placed his lips on hers. The sensation was instantaneous euphoria—walking along a beautiful beach or splashing in rain puddles along a country road. She accepted the passion of his touch and whispered into his mouth. "How do you like the wine?"

He jerked back from her, rose, and stalked across the room. "We can't do this. It's crazy."

"Not as crazy as a curse."

"And—" He shrugged his shoulders. "That proves you haven't one ounce of Irish blood running through your veins."

"That's ridiculous."

"No, it's not." He started for the stairs but turned back to her. "If you were Irish, you'd have no problem untangling the curse. But, sadly, you're not."

"Damn it, Ansel." Zoe jumped up from the sofa and shook her fist at him. "I'll show you how damned Irish I am, and I'll crack your stupid curse.

Chapter Five

A maddening noise woke Zoe from a dream. A pleasant dream where she strolled down a white beach with waves tickling her toes. A man held her hand, kissing the palm. She looked at him, hoping beyond hope he was her ghost, but she never saw his face because of the damned phone. She pried open an eye, the digital clock glared 3:17. She snagged the irritating device. "Hello."

"I'd like to request a song," someone said.

"What?"

"Is this Mix 95.6?"

"No!" Zoe slammed down the receiver. "I gotta get a new number," she muttered and rolled over.

Zoe slept through her alarm that Friday morning and raced to get ready for work. In the kitchen, she poured coffee while Ansel appeared at the bistro table.

"Good morning, Zoe. It's a beautiful day."

"Says who?"

"Didn't you sleep well?" His gaze ran up and down her body. "You don't look like you had a rough night. In fact, you're glowing."

"I'm fine." She watched Ansel over the rim of her cup, her anger from last night forgotten. He must have been a charmer in his day, handsome and a good sense of humor. Qualities a woman looked for in a man—a woman like Zoe. She shook the thought from her head.

How sad for him, being stuck in her house and not having true peace in his life after death. It wasn't fair to him, simply not fair at all. Other than the smart-ass streak and the clanging and banging, he wasn't all that bad. He deserved a better existence. He deserved closure on his death. He deserved to go to his grave, and she would help him get there. Not for the article, or to hasten his exit from her attic, but simply for his benefit, for his eternal peace. And she'd do it minus an Irish ancestry.

"I've made a decision," Zoe announced.

"Uh-oh."

"Don't worry, you'll like it." She grabbed her purse and started for the front door. "I'll liberate you from this house and send you to your final resting place."

He raised an eyebrow. "How are you going to do that?"

"Resolve the curse, Mr. Delaney.

∾

Mid-morning at the bookstore, Zoe ran into Mr. Allen at the coffee bar. They talked about the store's Halloween decorations and the weather, no mention of yesterday's due diligence. She was dying to ask him but she held back. No way would she let him see her nervousness.

But that didn't stop her from calling the business broker.

"Mr. Barry, I hope you can give me an update on

my offer for Merlin's."

"Good to hear from you. I'm waiting for the final proposal from the other party. Once I have that, I'll prepare a summary evaluating the two and present it to Mr. Allen."

She did not like this unexpected complication to her plans. "Is there anything else I can provide to strengthen my proposal?"

"No, no, everything is quite clear. We'll be ready for Mr. Allen to make a decision by the middle of next week."

"I'll keep my fingers crossed."

As soon as she hung up the phone, it rang.

"Darling, how are you today?" Aunt Tina sparkled as usual.

"I'm fine, just worried about my plans for Merlin's."

"You've done all you can do. If it's meant to happen, it will."

"I guess you're right."

"Of course I am." Aunt Tina never doubted herself. "I have news for you from Teddy."

"About what?"

"He gathered additional data for you from the library archives," Aunt Tina said.

"Excellent. Is it on the Dodd family?"

"Sure is. We have a list of names and a couple of addresses. Guess where part of the family settled?"

"No clue. Where?" Zoe was not good at and didn't like guessing games.

"New Orleans."

"Now, that's interesting." She hadn't been there

since one wild weekend during college. It was one of her favorite cities, or at least it had been. This information could kick off her plan to help Ansel. "Are you up for a road trip?"

"If you're talking about flying to New Orleans, I'm in."

"That's exactly what I'm talking about." She loved her aunt's adventurous streak. "Let's leave in the morning. I have a date tonight."

"I do as well. I'll make the reservations and call you later this afternoon. I'll also ask Teddy to fax the information he found."

Zoe grabbed a sandwich for lunch and sat at her desk making notes for Saturday's trip. Teddy's notes pointed out that Charlotte's uncle and his wife, Jack and Suzanne Dodd, had moved to New Orleans after World War II and started an insurance agency. Her own research had discovered Charlotte gave birth to a son in early 1939. She wondered if Uncle Jack had a relationship with her son. She added another item to her list of questions.

While jotting down her notes, Zoe's thoughts turned to Ansel. She smiled and closed her eyes for a moment, remembering their recent experience with the wine. She had enjoyed the-almost-kiss, and based on his reaction, he had too. But they couldn't do it again.

Once she solved the curse, he would be going home to his eternal resting place. Ansel very well might disagree with going to his grave, as he seemed very happy living in her attic. But what kind of life was that for him? Shouldn't dead people reside at their burial places?

Too bad he was a ghost and not human. She would love to kiss him for real.

~∽

Zoe made her usual Friday evening stop at the grocery store. The menu for her homemade meal for Sam was one of her favorite forty-five minute meals—lemon shrimp and pasta, green salad, and crusty bread.

While putting items in the refrigerator, she heard a whistle behind her. "Hey Ansel, what's up?" She turned around, and there he was, filling the doorway and looking damn near perfect. "You must have had a good day. You're looking very, uh, robust." Good enough to touch and hug.

"It was good." He flexed a bicep. "Yes, my day worked out well."

Zoe pulled out a large pot and the salad spinner. "What did you do?"

"Not much." He sat at the bistro table. "I love this table. It reminds me of the outdoor cafes in Rome. What's for dinner?"

"I'm cooking for Sam. Remember, I told you about him?" She tore lettuce for the salad.

"Guess I forgot." He sighed and crossed his long legs. "But I do remember you cooking with your Nana as a little girl, about nine or ten years old. You made brownies."

"You're kidding. I can't believe you remember that. You saw us?"

"Every move you made. You tried your best to copy your grandmother. The eggs crashing to the floor was a touching scene."

"Eggs?" She was puzzled for a moment, and then the memory of that long-ago day returned. "I tripped over my shoelace. I had taken a carton from the refrigerator and was carefully carrying it to the counter. So careful, in fact, that I didn't notice my tennis shoe was untied until I crashed to the faded pink linoleum."

"That's the way I remember it, too. I guess you inherited your love of cooking from your grandmother."

"She was wonderful about letting me help." Zoe filled the pasta pot with water. "What about you? Did you have a special grandparent?"

He nodded. "Mine was Granddad Mac, my mother's father, Aiden Fitzgerald McGregor."

"Irish?"

"You better believe it. He came to this country as a young child and thanked the lord every day of his life. He felt blessed to have the good fortune to live in a land with so much opportunity."

"Did he have any special abilities? You know, being Irish and all." Zoe had considered more than once that Ansel's curse might be a family tradition.

"He had a superb voice, a tenor." Ansel's eyes turned a blue more brilliant than usual as he spoke. "He and his brother used to give Sunday afternoon concerts after dinner. They were spectacular."

Mmm, did Granddad Mac have any other talents? Like being a warlock or a leprechaun? "Was he known for anything else?"

He winked at her. "You mean like casting spells with st—"

A train whistle screeched, circling the small kitchen and rattling the Italian plates on the wall. Zoe blinked once, then twice. Ansel had been sucked through a hole in the kitchen ceiling like a cartoon character exiting a room in a rush.

She stared at the smooth ceiling where he'd disappeared. "Holy shit. Guess the curse didn't like me asking questions about Ansel's family." She shook her fist at the ceiling. "This is far from over. Dumb curse."

∾

Sam placed his napkin on the kitchen table and patted his stomach. "Good dinner, my compliments to the chef."

"Thank you. Why don't we have our coffee outside?"

"Great idea." Sam sat with Zoe on her small patio, admiring the stars while holding a steaming mug of coffee. It had been a pleasant evening so far, good food and good conversation.

He couldn't recall the last time he had met a woman as open as Zoe. Her topics of conversation, from the value of the US dollar's impact on gas prices to her favorite music, were original. She had a genuineness about her that was refreshing. But that was immaterial. Sam wasn't looking for a girlfriend. His only reason for dating her was to discover the location of a rare book. She filled the role as the conduit to find it.

"Sam, I hope the coffee isn't too strong for you."

"No, it's fine. What else do you enjoy besides good coffee?"

"That's a big question," she said.

"I know you like to cook." Sam hoped she'd admit to having an appetite for rare books. And that might lead to the whereabouts of *Tom Sawyer*.

She sipped her coffee. "Mmm, other interests? I suppose reading is my favorite past time."

"Working in a bookstore makes sense then." Good, finally they were getting somewhere.

"I suppose it does," she said. "But like I told you before, I hope to own Merlin's."

"I heard about that. Are you close to completing the deal?" Sam starred at his shoes as a twinge of guilt surfaced. He pushed it back. Finding *The Adventure of Tom Sawyer* for his family came first. He owed it to his deceased father and his sister.

"I should hear next week. I hate to say it, but I wish the other party would just drop off the stratosphere." She shifted her gaze from the yard to Sam. "I feel like my whole life hedges on owning Merlin's."

The guilt knife wedged a little further into Sam's gut. He ignored it and again reminded himself, family first. He reached over and patted her hand. "Keep your chin up. I'm sure everything will be fine."

"Thanks. I sure hope so," she said quietly.

"Does Merlin's ever deal in rare or old books?"

"Funny you should ask that."

Sam's stomach muscles tightened. "Why's that?"

"Several months ago I brought home an old trunk full of books Mr. Allen said were old and out of print. I guess it got pushed aside with Nana's death and then moving here."

"What sort of books?"

"I never opened the trunk. Guess I ought to add that to my to-do list," she said and giggled. "It gets longer every day."

Sam hankered to ask the location of the trunk but held back. Spooking her wouldn't be smart. He glanced at his watch. "It's late. I should be heading out."

They walked around the side of the house and stood next to his car. Sam's guilt in using Zoe bubbled up, but he ignored it once again. He gave her a quick hug. "Your dinner was great." He kissed her softly on the lips and then pulled back. "I'd like to return the favor."

"Sure." She licked her lower lip.

Her reaction pleased him in spite of his vow to stay away from women who were girlfriend material. "I'll call you early next week, and we can set a date."

She nodded while Sam leaned in closer and placed his lips on her mouth. After a moment the kiss deepened, and their tongues touched. He pulled back slowly. "I better go. Thanks again for dinner."

"You're welcome," Zoe mumbled.

Neither Sam nor Zoe noticed the transparent shadow at the attic window behind them. Ansel knew his actions were childish, but he didn't trust this Sam character. The man gave off a foul stench. Yet Zoe had kissed the stinker, twice, so she wasn't aware of it. Ansel had to protect her. His stomach twisted and his fists clenched at the picture in his mind of Sam kissing her. "No rank human is going to hurt Zoe. I'll kill him first."

～◦～

Ansel found Zoe in the kitchen Saturday morning, her eyes focused on the window over the sink. A suitcase stood in the doorway.

"Afraid of forgetting your bag?" he asked. Why else would she leave it where it could easily be tripped over?

Zoe jerked before turning around.

"Damn it, Ansel. Stop doing that. Remember we agreed on whistling or clanging chains?"

"Sorry. I forget you can't hear me walk." Wouldn't that be spectacular if she could?

"Whatever. I'm in a hurry." Zoe poured coffee into her tall mug. "What's up?"

"Nothing. Are you going somewhere?" She'd spent every night at the house since she'd moved in, and he didn't want that to change.

"Aunt Tina and I are going to New Orleans this morning. We hope to contact some family members of Charlotte Dodd—"

"Charlotte!" He hadn't heard her name in decades. "I can't think of any family she has in New Orleans."

Zoe smiled. "They moved almost a decade after you died. Charlotte's Uncle Jack set up a home there after World War II and opened an insurance business."

"I remember him." Ansel was gratified he could recall a member of the Dodd family. "Nice man and a confirmed bachelor as I recall."

"Yeah, well, the war changed a lot of people. At least that's what Nana always said."

"Your Nana had many opinions. Anyone else you're looking up on your trip?" Ansel assumed Zoe was too practical to be going out of state to interview the descendants of only one family.

"There are a couple of other items on the list."

The volume on his radar turned to the screeching level. "What items?" he asked, rubbing his ear.

"Nothing much." She turned her back to him, pouring a glass of water.

"Zoe." His voice was louder than he intended.

Water splashed out of the glass. "Geez, you don't have to yell."

"Sorry. I, uh . . . was my killer ever caught and sent to prison?"

"No."

"As I suspected. This trip isn't a good idea." He doubted he could talk her out of it, but he sure would try to do so.

"That's ridiculous."

She had the gall to wink at him, which he ignored.

"No, it's not ridiculous. Think about it. Some seventy years after an unsolved murder, a cute and curious young woman from Houston starts asking questions." He rubbed a hand over his face. "Questions buried for over seven decades. Don't you think that might make someone unhappy?"

"I suppose. I hadn't thought of it like that. But don't worry, I'm a big girl." She folded a dish towel and laid it on the side of the sink. "I promise I'll be careful."

"Please do." Ansel had been racking his brain. How could the two of them stay in contact while she was in New Orleans? Damn. If only he could use a cell phone. That was the answer. "I have an idea."

"About what?"

"About how you could contact me if you have an emergency."

"An emergency? What would you do?"

"I don't know . . . call 911." He had to make her understand. "Please, humor an old ghost."

"Okay, okay." She fluttered her eyelashes. "What should I do if I need help?"

"Remember the other night when we mentally kissed?" She nodded and he continued. "I think we should try the same technique. If you need to contact me, think of your home phone number and then imagine me answering the phone."

"That's all?"

"That's my best guess. I think it'll work." He had his fingers crossed behind his back.

"Let's hope I don't need to try it out." Zoe looked at her watch. "I need to run." She grabbed the coffee and rolled the bag to the front door. He trailed behind her. "Ansel, stay out of trouble. No programming the DVR, and don't try to drink any wine. I'll be home Sunday afternoon. Okay?"

"I'm not a six-year-old." Damn. He had planned on trying the DVR again. "Have a good trip." At the front window he watched her back out of the driveway. "Safe wings, my love."

He returned to the attic and his rocking chair. The creaking echoed throughout the empty house. He thought about Zoe kissing Sam last night, and his fists clenched. She sure seemed to enjoy it. He wanted so badly to punch something. He had little power to do so, but he wasn't helpless or without determination.

He rose and began to run in place. His legs were

weak and wobbly, and his knees kept turning east and west rather than pointing north. He kept at it and concentrated on raising his feet up and down and pumping his arms at his sides. After fifteen minutes he got the hang of it and found his groove for the next two hours. Time suspended as all he could think about was his housemate.

Ansel realized he was in love with her. It was ridiculous. He hardly knew Zoe in a person-to-person way. And to make it worse, she didn't have a chance in hell of resolving the curse and helping him pass to his rightful station in life. His bragging about coming up with a "plan" to help her had come to nothing, a big fat zero. He was almost helpless, and she might be in danger in New Orleans. Surely there was something he could do. He had to pull his wits together and think— think about the best way to go about the task. He froze in place.

After a moment he snapped his fingers and returned to the rocking chair. He had the best idea of all time—how he could help Zoe. And maybe, just maybe, she would realize that he was a ghost with the potential of being the man she would love for all eternity. He pumped his fist up and down. Yeah, baby, he finally had it going right for once.

∾↦

Interstate 45 North sucked, even on a Saturday morning. Zoe vowed to petition the state legislature to ban eighteen-wheelers from Texas freeways during daylight hours. After the second near collision with one traveling at a dangerous speed, she moved to the far right lane and slowed down. Bush International

Airport was only five miles ahead, so she had plenty of time.

Her cell phone rang. Surely Ansel hadn't already figured out how to use a cell phone.

"Hi, baby."

"Mom, you're home." Guess he hadn't figured it out.

"We arrived late last night. And, yes, before you ask, Paris was magnificent. We enjoyed every minute of our tour."

"I'm glad you're home. I missed you guys."

"How are you, sweetheart? And what are you and Tina up to?" Zoe's mother was the opposite of Aunt Tina, proving that twins weren't always two peas in a pod. Yet the two sisters still had that indisputable twin connection.

"Mom, I'm fine, and why are you asking what I'm up to?" She swore her mother had ESP. She always knew what Zoe was doing and with whom. It had been a significant handicap as a teenager. Forget those typical pranks. No way. Mama Toni never failed to uncover them.

"Oh, you know me, just a feeling. What's going on?"

"Nothing. I'm waiting to hear about my offer for Merlin's. A second party made an offer, so that's complicated things."

"Keep your chin up. If it's meant to be, your offer will prevail." As well as being annoyingly psychic, Zoe's mother always had good advice.

"Thanks, Mom. Say a prayer for me."

"You better believe it. By the way, I'll expect you

at dinner tomorrow evening. You can tell us all about your visit to New Orleans. Oh, I need to hang up. Your father's waiting."

She clicked off. Aunt Tina must have blabbed their plans. Typical. The sisters couldn't keep anything from each other. Zoe hoped to have an interesting story to tell her parents tomorrow, and one subject she would not mention was her overzealous interest in Ansel.

That reminded her of his concern for her safety in New Orleans. So sweet. He intended to take care of her as best he could. Yes, sweet, but ridiculous and unnecessary.

Chapter Six

Zoe and Aunt Tina arrived at their rental car within thirty minutes of the plane touching down in New Orleans. It had to be a record. They stowed their luggage in the trunk and set off for the exit from the lot.

Zoe drove a short distance between the rows of cars, stopped at a cross street. A traffic sign indicated a right-hand turn to exit the airport. She carefully looked to the left, no oncoming traffic, and began a slow turn to the right. Suddenly, a white SUV with a blaring horn rushed down the lane in front of their small red sedan.

"Where did that guy come from? He missed us by barely six inches." Aunt Tina said.

"He came out of nowhere." Zoe watched the vehicle barrel out of the rental lot. "Crazy people. I'll be extra careful driving here."

They soon headed east on Interstate 10 toward downtown New Orleans and the Bourbon Riverview Hotel. The traffic was light, so Zoe guessed there were no footballs games that weekend. After a few minutes on the interstate, Zoe noticed an SUV that had been behind them for several miles. At first, it was two or three car lengths behind them, and then it was almost glued to their bumper. Then it backed off again. This action repeated two or three times.

"Aunt Tina, look behind us. Is that white SUV the same car that nearly ran into us when we exited the rental lot?"

She turned and looked out the back window.

"Maybe, I only noticed it was white. It's getting awfully close." She glanced at Zoe. "Why don't you speed up a bit, and we'll see what it does?"

Zoe pressed on the gas, ever mindful of driving on an unfamiliar freeway. "What's the SUV doing now?" She looked in the rearview mirror. "It's still behind us."

"Jerks," Tina muttered. "Try slowing down. That usually frustrates crazy drivers and they'll go around."

After a few seconds at the slower pace, the SUV roared past them and disappeared around a curve ahead.

"You were right." Zoe let out a shaky breath. "It's gone. Take a look at the map. What exit do we take to get to the hotel?"

Tina pulled out the driving directions provided by the rental agency. "We need to turn right on Canal Street. But we still have a few miles to go before we reach the exit."

"Got it, exit at Canal Street," Zoe said.

Tina nodded.

They rode in silence for a minute or two.

Suddenly, Tina pointed toward the driver's window of the car. "Don't look now, Zoe, but I think the white SUV is back."

Zoe quickly glanced to her left. "I couldn't see anyone in the front seat. The windows are too dark." What's going on? Someone following them in New Orleans didn't make sense. She tightened her grip on the steering wheel and punched the gas pedal.

"Be careful, sweetheart." Tina made sure the car's doors were locked.

Within seconds the SUV hugged the edge of the lane and veered in their direction. The two vehicles were less than a foot apart.

"What a jackass," Tina exclaimed.

"He's trying to run us off the road," Zoe shouted. The SUV swerved closer to the rented sedan at sixty miles an hour. She looked in the rearview mirror. No vehicles were behind her. "Hold on. I'm going to brake."

She slammed hard on the brake pedal, pumped it a few times, and guided the car to the shoulder.

"My God, is that guy nuts?" Tina cried and pointed toward the windshield. "Look, Zoe. He's pulling over, too."

"Yeah, like he's playing with us."

"Why is he doing this? Did we cut him off or something? Road rage?"

Zoe watched the white SUV. It idled about a hundred feet in front of them on the shoulder. The back-up lights came on.

"Aunt Tina, he's backing up."

"I see that. We should call 911. I'll get my phone." Tina reached to the backseat for her purse and noticed a police car pulling up behind them with its lights flashing. "We've got company."

Zoe glanced in the side mirror. "I see it." Her gaze lifted to the windshield. "There goes the SUV."

It roared down the freeway, crossing left over a couple of lanes. Within seconds it was gone from their sight.

The patrol officer knocked on the driver's side window. Zoe explained they had stopped to make a phone call, safety first. He accepted the explanation, wished them a good day, and a few moments later the patrol car back slid back into the traffic.

"Let's wait a few minutes before we start again." Zoe needed the break for her nerves to settle down.

"Good idea." Aunt Tina searched Zoe's face. "Any guess who was in the SUV?"

"Not right now."

"You know, it might be related to our trip here. Not some random road rage. But that's awfully far-fetched." Aunt Tina sounded doubtful.

"I agree. Only Teddy and Ansel, and my parents, knew we were coming. Who would they tell?" Zoe answered her own question. "No one."

The next fifteen minutes passed in silence. Zoe exited off Interstate 10 at Canal Street and turned right toward the Mississippi River. After a few blocks, they reached the French Quarter.

Aunt Tina named the streets they passed. "Bourbon, Royal, St. Charles. The Quarter is just as I remember it. Full of people out for a good time."

Zoe checked her watch. "We have about an hour and a half before our appointment this afternoon. Why don't we check into the hotel and grab a cup of coffee? Or are you hungry?'

"No. I'm saving my calories for dinner." Aunt Tina laughed. "Let's get settled first. Then you can fill me in on the plan for our meeting."

Zoe glanced at her aunt with a half-smile.

"I don't want to say anything wrong, sweetheart. You know how my mouth can run away from good sense when I get excited."

Zoe laughed. "I have a feeling this won't be the exciting sort of discussion. I just hope Mrs. Ford will open up to us."

"Harrah's Casino is up and running," Aunt Tina exclaimed. "Too bad we don't have more time. I'd love to play the slots or poker."

"Another visit, Auntie." Zoe chuckled. Her aunt definitely had a fun side to her personality.

Just past Harrah's, the Bourbon Riverview Hotel came into view on their right. Zoe swung into the small circular driveway of the hotel, parking at the valet stand.

They checked in, dropped off their luggage in the room, and made a beeline for the hotel's Crescent City Café and cups of strong Louisiana coffee. Zoe studied a street map of New Orleans, plotting the quickest route between the hotel and the Dodd family house in the Garden District.

"It'll probably be easy to find the house," Aunt Tina commented. "I think the streets are well laid out, not like Houston."

"You're right. I like to have a mental picture of the streets."

"Is your picture ready then? I'd like to look at some of the houses if we have time." To make her point, Aunt Tina stood and gathered her purse and sweater. "Are you ready?"

"All righty then, let's go." Zoe followed her aunt to the car. "I hope we learn something to solve the curse. Otherwise I may have a ghost in the attic until I'm ready to join him." Zoe shivered. What a terrible thought.

Within a few minutes, they arrived at the north edge of the Garden District. Decades old trees outlined the streets and divided them as well, marching along wide esplanades. Although it was early October, they were still full of leaves, providing generous shade to the surrounding lawns.

The gardens were spectacular. They overflowed with rainbows of color and provided a magical overcoat to the view of the houses from the street. Thanks to a college course on architectural styles, Zoe recognized Greek Revival, Georgian, and Victorian homes as she slowly wound through the area.

"These magnificent homes are worth the trip," Aunt Tina remarked

"I agree. The history here is priceless." Zoe nodded at the paper lying on the car's center console. "Could you give me the address of the Dodd house?"

"It's 115 First Street. The cross street is Chestnut."

"We just passed First. I'll circle back around."

They easily located the Dodd house and parked in front along the street. The house was built in the Greek Revival style and was massive—three stories set back from the street with a beautifully landscaped lawn. A stone fountain with a water goddess and urn spilling water graced the center lawn with beds of blooming red and white flowers on either side.

Zoe rang the doorbell and reassured herself she had a solid plan to approach the topic of Ansel's curse. She figured going slow and easing her way toward it would work better than blurting it out.

The door opened, revealing a petite, expertly made-up blonde woman.

"Mrs. Ford?"

"Yes, I'm Sara Ford."

"I'm Zoe Miller, and this is my aunt, Tina Peters."

"Please come in." She motioned for them to enter the house.

"Thank you for seeing us on such short notice." Zoe followed her aunt into a two-story foyer dominated by a crystal chandelier. Mrs. Ford's heels clicked on the marble floor as she led them to a room off to the right, a sitting room or parlor. The room was elegantly decorated with plush sage carpets, oak-paneled walls, and an artful collection of yellow silk sofas and chairs. Mrs. Ford led them to matching sofas separated by a thick glass coffee table.

"I thought you might enjoy a glass of wine. After all, this is News Orleans." Mrs. Ford pulled a bottle from a silver wine cooler on the table and poured three glasses. "This is a Reserve Chardonnay bottled especially for the Ford family." She handed a glass to Tina and then one to Zoe. "Salud."

Zoe tasted the wine, stealing a quick glance at Aunt Tina, who didn't seem at all surprised by drinking wine at one o'clock in the afternoon.

"Excellent wine, Mrs. Ford, a New Orleans tradition I could get accustomed to," Zoe said. "Your home is lovely. I'm sure it has an interesting history being in the Garden District."

"Does it have a ghost, by any chance?" Aunt Tina asked.

"As a matter of fact, it does. Would you like to hear the story?" Mrs. Ford's eyes glowed as she clutched her hands together on her lap.

"Yes, please," Zoe replied. She was eager to hear about another ghost.

"The spirit's name is Julia. She was a fifteen-year-old girl who loved a young man her parents disapproved of, the typical story of young love. After the Christmas Eve festivities of 1904, she attempted an escape from her bedroom to meet him. She fell while climbing out the window and broke her neck. Naturally, she blames her parents for her death and continues to irritate adults as best she can."

"My heavens, that's incredible. Have you seen her yourself?" Tina said.

"Yes, many times, usually around her birthday and Christmas Eve. She expects us to remember her on those days and gets angry if we don't," Mrs. Ford said, a gentle smile on her lips. "Tell me about your ghost. I assume it's Ansel, since you asked about the curse when you called yesterday."

"Yes, it's Ansel," Tina said, glancing at her niece. "He resides in Zoe's attic."

"Ah, you own the house he was murdered in."

Zoe took a deep breath and blew it out slowly, clenched and unclenched her fists. "Yes, I'm the owner. I inherited it a few months ago from my grandmother. She and my grandfather bought it from

Charlotte Dodd in 1941."

"That would have been a couple of years after Charlotte and Maxim married. I think she initially wanted to hold onto the house in case her marriage didn't work out."

"Did you know Charlotte?" Zoe asked.

"She was my favorite aunt. We all loved her. She was full of fun and loved to play games. Plus she always had a joke or funny story to tell."

"She sounds great. Your families visited often then?" Zoe knew in her gut, minus any concrete evidence, that someone in either the Dodd or Delaney family held the key to unlocking the curse.

"We were together almost every holiday. My grandmother, Suzanne Dodd, Charlotte's older sister, and Lucy Whitmire, Ansel's mother, were best friends." Mrs. Ford smiled. "Their friendship brought the two families together often, either here or in Houston."

"Sounds like a blast," Zoe said.

"Exactly." Mrs. Ford topped off their wineglasses. "The two women were so close that for over forty years they shared their diaries or 'my private thoughts' as Granny Suz called hers."

"What a wonderful example of a close friendship between women," Tina remarked. "It's amazing how long it lasted."

"Their relationship raised the craziness level when the families were together. My cousin, Robert Delaney, and I had loads of fun together." Mrs. Ford must have noticed the question in Zoe's eyes. "He was Charlotte and Maxim's natural child. He's now the head of the family business."

Geez, another member of the Delaney family. Zoe needed a chart to keep up with everyone. How sad that poor Ansel never had a chance to know his nephew. Hmm, how many others in his family had he missed knowing? No doubt he would have been in the middle of the fun, like his mother and Granny Suz. Of course, his mother did seem on the strange side. Case in point, placing a curse on her favorite child wasn't normal.

Why in the hell would a mother do such a thing? Zoe's mother had said many times that there is no love greater than that of a mother for her children. Lucy must have had a good reason for placing a curse on Ansel—"mom knows best," right? *Must have been one hell of a good reason*. Maybe she blamed Ansel for his death and that prompted the curse. Whatever the reason, Lucy was one weird mother. Poor Ansel.

Zoe shook her head and found both Aunt Tina and Mrs. Ford watching her. She ran a hand through her hair and then sipped her wine, gaining a moment to regroup her wandering thoughts.

"May I ask a couple of questions about the curse placed on Ansel?" Zoe had to know the truth. Why was Ansel stuck in her attic?

"Of course," Mrs. Ford replied.

"He told me—"

"You've talked with him?" Mrs. Ford pressed a hand over her mouth.

"Several times. He's helping me write an article on ghosts being stuck in the place of their deaths," Zoe said.

Mrs. Ford sipped her wine and inspected Zoe over

the top of the glass. "How very, very interesting."

"I guess," she said, shrugging. "Anyway, he told me he couldn't outright tell me why he's still in my house. I have to figure it out myself."

"We discovered the curse in his mother's diaries," Aunt Tina added.

"How in the world did you come across Lucy's diaries?" Mrs. Ford asked as her eyes widened.

"We found them at the Houston Public Library," Aunt Tina explained while a faint blush crept up her face. "A good friend of mine is the director there."

"I see," Mrs. Ford said.

"But they didn't provide much information about the curse. Pages were missing. I'm curious why Mrs. Whitmire would curse her own son. Also, how did she do it, and how can it be erased or reversed?" Zoe crossed her fingers. "I'd be so grateful if you could give us any information, any at all."

"I'm sorry. I can't talk about the details of the curse to anyone outside the family. After all, both my grandmother's and Lucy's diaries are private."

"Please, can't you make an exception this one time? I need to help Ansel." Zoe had to make her understand. "He deserves to be free and, uh, pass to his grave. He should have been there the past seventy years and not stuck in a dusty old attic."

Zoe watched Mrs. Ford as she weighed the impact of the question. Surely, she debated whether the opportunity to help Ansel was worth allowing an outsider to learn intimacies of his family's history. Mrs. Ford emptied her wineglass. From the determined look on her face, she had made a decision.

"I'll help you," Mrs. Ford said, raising a hand. "But realize the information I can provide is limited."

Zoe mentally jumped up and down. "Anything you tell us will be helpful."

Mrs. Ford aimed a smile at Zoe. "I'll tell you why the curse was placed on Ansel. However, I can't explain why or how it was placed or the method for removal."

Zoe and Aunt Tina said in unison, "Oh, okay."

Mrs. Ford's gaze traveled from Zoe to Aunt Tina, and then she clarified, "The method of resolution you'll have to discover on your own. Fair enough?"

"Yes, ma'am, we do appreciate anything you can tell us," Zoe replied. She had complete faith in her ability to solve the curse once she knew how it had been placed. Seriously, neutralizing a seventy-year-old curse shouldn't be all that difficult. Any almost thirty-year-old woman who could kiss a ghost could solve a curse.

True to her word, Mrs. Ford provided the details explaining that Mrs. Whitmire placed the curse on Ansel in anger. She believed he did something to cause his own murder, and she wanted to get back at him. Definitely not a motherly gesture, but as the years passed she regretted her decision. Over time, and through many rounds of family gossip, most members of the Dodd and Delaney families knew of the curse.

"Has anyone in the family had contact with Ansel since he died?" Zoe asked.

"Aunt Charlotte is the only one I'm aware of. The story is that he appeared in her bedroom, the room where he died, on the eve of her wedding to Maxim."

"Incredible." Tina leaned forward. "Was he against the wedding?"

"Most definitely. The family gossip is that Ansel was convinced Maxim didn't love her. After several years of dating, he abruptly broke up with her. The scuttlebutt was that he wasn't ready to settle down. Granny Suz always said Maxim was simply too immature to have a wife."

"But they married anyway," Tina pointed out.

"Charlotte wanted a father for Ansel's son."

"What?" Zoe exclaimed. "Ansel had a son?"

"Well, yes. I assumed that's why you were interested in the curse. Once Lucy discovered Ansel, not Maxim, was the father of Charlotte's son, she tried over and over to release the curse."

Tina's face scrunched up for a moment. "I don't have children myself, but I can't imagine a mother acting like Lucy. Surely she had some type of mental, uh, incapacity."

"Ansel's murder was a turning point for her," Mrs. Ford said. "She was never the same after his death."

"Did Lucy ever discover who killed Ansel?" Zoe said.

"If she did, the family wasn't told," she replied. "But yes, I believe that after a time she knew exactly who was responsible for her son's death."

∾∽

Forest Lawn Cemetery, Houston, 1938

Thud. Plop. Plop. Plop.

A shiny shovel dropped Texas dirt mixed with caliche clay on the rich mahogany of Ansel's casket. Drops of rain followed, chasing mourners to their vehicles. Lucy Whitmire didn't melt. Planted under a hastily opened umbrella, she stood next to her second husband, William Whitmire.

How could a mother live through, no, suffer through the aftermath of her darling child dying a premature death? A death that wasn't paid for, a death without accountability. A death that broke a mother's heart and bankrupted her soul.

For now Lucy accepted the broken heart and reacted to the ever-present pain without thinking. The funeral service and burial of her son, Ansel, were without parallel, the most traumatic events of her life. The loss of a husband was one thing, but the early loss of the favorite child was something entirely different. Ansel's death was so horrendous she couldn't venture beyond the pain.

Lucy stared at the spray of white roses resting on top of the casket. He loved, no had loved, white roses. He had given them to her for every Mother's Day since he had turned twenty-one. Now she would give them to him.

Her thoughts turned to Ansel's father. The fool had been too old to ride jumpers and died five years earlier in a senseless riding accident. The son followed the father in such foolishness. What had Ansel done to get himself killed? She knew in her soul it hadn't been an accident. No. Ansel was at fault. He had to be. Delaney's didn't get murdered without good reason. Her precious boy had gotten himself into some type of trouble. Damn him. Damn him to hell.

Lucy glanced at the faces of the family and friends attending the burial service—sadness, tears, and low spirits. She would set Ansel straight for causing so much pain. Yes, she'd teach her favorite son a much-needed lesson, even in death.

Later in the day, Lucy was alone in her bedroom. It smelled of her favorite and expensive French perfume. The normally pleasant fragrance angered her now. It roused the unpleasant memory of flowers overflowing Ansel's casket earlier that day. The memory once again roused her anger.

She moved to a cherry chest, about the size of a cigar box, sitting on a lace doily placed in the middle of her vanity table. She stared at the container, uncertain of why she stood before it.

After a moment of silent reflection, she gently raised the unadorned lid. Her hand snaked in to recover a small object. It was hidden in her palm while she moved to the antique rocking chair waiting for her in front of the fireplace. Although the season was warm, a meager fire tried to thaw the ice surrounding her heart.

Lucy rubbed the blue-marbled, egg-shaped stone with her thumb. The stone's surface was smooth and comforting. Surprisingly, it calmed her nerves and guided her course of action.

"Oh, stone of power, hear my plea. Grant me this curse for eternity, unless the love of a human interrupts its power. Only then will the recipient of the curse be brought back to life."

Chapter Seven

After a backyard tour of the family garden, Mrs. Ford offered a quick trip to the family cemetery. It was only a few blocks away, so how could they pass up the opportunity to see a New Orleans' graveyard up close and personal? Zoe questioned Mrs. Ford's spontaneous offer, wondering if the woman had a hidden motive. Then she questioned her own sanity for jumping to conclusions about someone she hardly knew. Time would tell, as Nana always said.

It was a five-minute drive through the Garden District to the Lafayette 2 Cemetery. They parked along Camp Street and entered through an aging wrought iron gate.

Mrs. Ford led them along a cracked path bordered by bleached aboveground vaults to a small area housing the family tombs. She explained that the Dodd's, including Charlotte, were located in the family section. Aunt Tina commented that the faceplates on the vaults, gray or black granite, were hard to read.

Zoe stood before Charlotte's grave—born in 1914, died in 2000, devoted mother and friend forever, end of story. It seemed strange there was no hint of Maxim as the faithful spouse. How interesting that Charlotte wasn't buried next to her husband. Where was he laid to rest? It did seem unusual for man and wife to be split up after death. It said what needed to be said about Charlotte and Maxim's marriage, or lack of a marriage.

Mrs. Ford stood before her grandmother's vault, smiling.

"Do you visit her often?" Zoe asked.

"About once a month." Mrs. Ford turned at Zoe's approaching steps. "I like to check on the vaults. Make sure there hasn't been any vandalism."

"Everything looks good," Zoe replied. "I was wondering. Why is Charlotte buried here? I don't see a marker for Maxim."

Mrs. Ford shrugged. "Personal choice, I suppose. Maxim's grave is in Houston. We all agreed it was unusual, but I think she felt closer to the Dodd family than the Delaney's. She often referred to herself as Charlotte Dodd even after she married Maxim." She bent down, pulled a couple of weeds from the narrow strip of grass surrounding her grandmother's aboveground vault. "And it says everything about the quality of their marriage. Don't you think?"

Both Zoe and Aunt Tina nodded.

She continued, "I can't imagine burial anywhere but next to my husband."

Zoe moved down the sidewalk a few feet and sat on a weathered cement bench. Aunt Tina and Mrs. Ford continued to talk.

Her mind wandered as she gazed off, admiring the variety of vaults. She wasn't sure if they were above ground due to two hundred years of Spanish and

French traditions entrenched in New Orleans society or because of the high water table of a city below sea level.

The vaults looked like faded white cubes of various heights and widths haphazardly scattered around the cemetery grounds. A few here and there had a bit of grass around their exterior or a potted plant in front. Overall, the vaults looked aged, weatherworn, and, well, past their prime.

She was certain Ansel's gravesite wasn't a vault. Would he be happy in a grave after spending seventy years in an attic? At least he'd finally be free in the ground, free as a ghost rather than as a human. She hoped all the research on the curse would help him pass to the other side. And getting him out of the attic would allow her to redecorate, not that it was all that important. She glanced at Aunt Tina and Mrs. Ford, who had moved farther down the sidewalk. She stretched her legs and pointed her face toward the warmth of the October sun.

"Have you learned anything useful yet?" Ansel lounged next to her on the bench, grinning his ass off.

Startled, she looked away to reconcile her surprise at seeing him in the sunshine. Luckily, she didn't do anything outlandish like jump up and down and scream her head off. Rather, she narrowed her eyes, appraising him. "Why is it you can show up here but not leave my attic? I wasn't even thinking of my home phone number."

"It's a natural spirit gift, and this is a cemetery. You were thinking of home." He copied her pose by stretching out his legs and raising his face to the sun.

"It's so rare these days that I feel the warmth of the sun."

Zoe gazed at him in exasperation. "Shouldn't the sun melt you or something?"

He moved his mouth to her ear and whispered, "Special powers."

"Whatever." She threw him a scathing look. "Tell me why you're really here."

"Just wanted to see how your research is going." He grinned again and pointed toward the burial vaults. "Learn anything useful from all those . . . dead people?"

She wondered how a ghost could be so cute and so irritating at the same time. Special powers, indeed.

"No, I haven't learned a thing. It's just interesting." She shooed him away with her hands. "Now, go away. I don't want to be caught talking to the empty air."

"That wouldn't do at all." Ansel rose and looked down at Zoe. "Before I leave, is there anything I can do to help you?"

"Sure. Tell me how to resolve the curse."

"Sorry, no can do." He evaporated without a puff of hot air to verify he had, five seconds earlier, lounged next to her on the bench.

She stared into space. What the hell was the problem with that ghost? One minute he was sweet and sexy, and the next minute he acted like a jerk. How inconsistent could one ghost be? If he didn't leave her home and life soon, he'd pull her further into his world. She intended to devote all her efforts to solving the curse. Afterwards, he'd be gone, and her life would finally be back on track. She rose, rolled her shoulders, and felt a hundred times better.

Although . . . she did enjoy having him at home. It was like having a roommate without all the usual drama. She'd never lived with a man before, well, a ghost-man. For a second she had a crazy idea—after she solved his murder and the curse, Ansel could simply stay living in her attic. What would it hurt? She stood, flipping a hand in front of her chest. No . . . that wasn't a good idea. It was unfair to Ansel. He deserved to live where he belonged, in his grave, surrounded by the rest of his family.

Zoe joined her aunt and Mrs. Ford near the entry gate of the cemetery. "Are we ready to get on our way?"

They dropped Mrs. Ford off at her front walk, and expressed their gratitude for the information Mrs. Ford had provided.

Once Zoe drove away from the curb, Aunt Tina spoke softly, "You won't believe what Mrs. Ford told me while you were on that bench throwing your arms around."

"What?"

"I think I know how to release the curse."

~⌒~

"Robert, what a pleasure to hear from you." Sara Ford removed a pearl earring. "How's everything in Houston?"

"Fine, just fine." His deep voice radiated through the receiver. "Anything new or interesting down your way?"

"No, we're still planning on hosting Thanksgiving

this year."

"We're all planning on driving down," he replied with a small laugh. "I hear Harrah's is fully operational again. I'll be playing some baccarat.

"I'm sure you won't be the only one." Sara smiled, remembering Robert's reputation among the families as the most prolific gambler. "I almost forgot. I had a visit with a young woman from Houston today, Zoe Miller. She's the one I mentioned in the e-mail yesterday."

"I vaguely recall something about her call to you. What was her reason for traveling to New Orleans?"

"She owns the house where Ansel Delaney died. She read about the curse and was curious about it— something about writing a magazine article on spirits in homes."

"I hope you didn't tell her anything. It's a private matter."

"Robert, we've been over this before. It's part of Houston's history. Don't forget, she learned about the curse from the public library."

He hesitated before speaking. "I suppose you're right, just as long as you didn't reveal anything that isn't already public."

"I may have accidentally given her one small piece of private information—"

"Damn it, Sara. This is unacceptable."

～⌒

The creaking of the rocking chair beat a matching rhythm to the nonstop drumming of rain against the attic window. It had been a miserable afternoon, matching Ansel's mood.

His brain was now working on all cylinders and had failed to produce the step-by-step strategy to instigate his big idea to help Zoe. The lack of one created a one-word result—loser.

Being a loser was so unlike him in his previous breathing state. Ansel had always prided himself on being the "idea guy" at J&L Manufacturing. The go-to guy when events required a shaking up or two. "Stirring the pot" had been necessary often after his father's death. Many of the older employees weren't fond of taking orders from the much less experienced son of the deceased owner. After many months of hard work and convincing J&L's executive staff, as well as every foreman, of his abilities, he had prevailed. Ansel had planned to announce an alliance with a German company, scheduled for two days after his murder. He wondered whether the agreement had been signed. And who was running J&L today? If the company still existed, that was. How could he find out?

The rocking chair continued to squeak as Ansel pondered this new dilemma. What would Zoe do? Damn it. Why was he even thinking about her? She created nothing but turmoil and regret in his "life." Regret that he was dead and no longer a man, and regret that he cared for her and couldn't act on it. He'd had a crush on her since . . . well, since Zoe was in college. She would visit her grandmother once a week for cooking and gardening.

One time Zoe had brought a lemon tree for the backyard. The two of them planted it in the corner of the bed along the fence. They used a garden hose to water the new tree and then kneeled on the grass next to it and said something, perhaps a plant prayer of some sort.

Living in the house with Nana had been easy. But now he was over his head in drama. Drama that he, and of course his mother, were largely responsible for. Damn it. He couldn't figure out a way to help Zoe with her article without making her life worse. If he did help her, he would be ensuring his eternity in hell.

Dinner at Brennan's in the French Quarter followed the trip to the Garden District. Seated in the courtyard while enjoying a glass of merlot, Zoe read the restaurant's history from the back of the menu. Opened in 1910, it had made "Banana's Foster" a dessert both envied and copied. Zoe made a mental note to order it and beg for the recipe at the end of the meal.

Aunt Tina commented on the weather, the beautiful azalea's surrounding the outdoor dining area, and the cute butt of their handsome waiter. She figured she had waited long enough.

"Okay, Auntie dear, time to talk. Tell me what Mrs. Ford told you at the cemetery that was so momentous." Zoe looked her aunt square in the eye. "Come on, fess up."

Tina sipped her chardonnay, raised her face upward. The lights in the courtyard provided a backdrop for the stars twinkling in the clear evening sky. She closed her eyes for a moment, no doubt weighing her words, and addressed her niece with a sly look on her face.

"I've given some thought to what Mrs. Ford said,

and now I'm not sure it will help you."

"Tell me anyway." Patience was not one of Zoe's strengths. "I want to know."

"She told me that love was a major part of resolving the curse."

"What? Love? That's all?"

"I believe the exact words were 'falling in love,' and then she stopped talking midsentence. I got the feeling she had said too much."

"Too much?"

"Yes, like she had revealed a secret. It was the look on her face— distressed is the only word I can think of to describe it." Tina finished her wine, signaled to the waiter for a refill.

"Distressed because resolving the curse means he falls in love." Zoe finished her wine as well. "Ansel and love, now that's an interesting combination. Maybe the curse evaporates if he falls in love." A tingle flushed Zoe's chest and neck before she recognized the humor in her words. "What a trip. To send the ghost in my attic to his grave, I must find him a girlfriend."

The arrival of their entrees interrupted the conversation. Aunt Tina glanced from her filet mignon to the shrimp salad in front of Zoe.

"Saving calories?"

"You bet. I'm ordering dessert."

Half an hour later, they engaged in complete decadence with Banana's Foster and enjoyed the finest of New Orleans coffee, with chicory, of course.

"Aunt Tina, assuming the falling in love idea does refer to Ansel, do you suppose the other party is someone from his past? Another spirit? Maybe Charlotte is floating around waiting to jump his bones."

"Why Charlotte?"

"Duh. He's the father of her first child. She didn't exactly have a love affair with her husband."

"Good point." Tina signed the check, and stood. "Come on, let's walk a bit. The fresh air will clear your mind."

The French Quarter was busy. Tourists carrying plastic cups of their favorite beverage strolled along the streets searching for the perfect watering hole. Zoe hardly noticed them. Her thoughts bounced from the truck that had tried to run them off the freeway to Sara Ford and the family history she had revealed. It was all so confusing.

"Why are we here, Aunt Tina?" she asked. "I feel like I'm going in circles. All I want to do is to buy Merlin's."

"Sweet pea, relax. We're in the Big Easy." Tina pointed down the street. "See that tarot card sign ahead. Let's stop in there. I haven't had a reading in years."

Zoe studied her aunt for a moment, shook her head. Life sure had a strange way of throwing distractions. "Why not? It can't be any worse than living with a crazy ghost."

Aunt Tina gave her niece a sharp look. "Watch your attitude, little missy. Life could be much worse."

"Sorry, you're right. I'm feeling a slight loss of control."

With a hand flat against the front door of the Miss

Marie's Tarot Shop, Tina looked back at Zoe, smiling sweetly. "You really need to get over that control thing."

Zoe rolled her eyes and followed her aunt into the shop.

The interior was dark except for a center table brightened by candles placed behind a person sitting at the table. As they entered the interior of the shop, a throaty voice called out.

"May I help you, ladies?"

Tina marched to the table. "Yes, you may. We'd both like a reading."

"Wonderful. I'm Madam Larue." She glanced from Zoe to Tina, then back to Zoe. Her green eyes sent mini lightning bolts across the room. "Who desires the first reading?" Tina raised her hand. "Please, sit in front of me." Madam Larue gestured to Zoe. "You may sit over there, out of the way."

Zoe parked herself as directed and zoned out. Naturally, her thoughts turned to Ansel and his appearance at the cemetery. How cool if his ghost magic transformed him back into a man. She sighed, made duck lips, and crossed her legs. That would never happen, him being dead, dead as a doornail. She giggled at the cliché. Maybe she needed another glass of merlot.

She had no idea how much time had passed before she noticed her aunt waving a hand in front of her face.

"Earth to Zoe, are you okay?'

"I'm fine, just thinking."

"Good. It's your turn for a reading, my treat."

She had no need for a tarot card reading but would

go along with the ordeal to make her aunt happy. "I'm ready."

They exchanged chairs, and she studied the woman across the table. Madam Larue had long blonde hair, a round face, dark eyes, and was dressed in some sort of flowing robe. Her age was undeterminable. She shuffled the cards, placed the deck on the scared tabletop in front of Zoe.

"Cut the cards, please."

Zoe did as instructed and scooted back on the hard seat of the folding chair to watch the show. She didn't believe in the magic of tarot cards and knew the reading was a fake. No one in their right mind would believe a deck of cards could accurately predict a person's future.

Fifteen minutes later, Zoe and Aunt Tina exited the shop back onto Royal Street. Zoe's head was swimming with the details of Madam Larue's reading. It was too much for her to process. She looked at her aunt, sensing a profound comment on the horizon.

"Zoe, that was incredible. I can't believe she said—"

Zoe raised her hand to stop her aunt's words. "Please, I need time to think about what she said. It's simply too off the wall. Who would believe it?"

～◌～

After donning flannel pajamas and washing her face, Zoe plopped in front of the television for the late-night news.

What a crazy day. It had started with Ansel questioning her sanity in going to New Orleans then followed by some jerk trying to run their car off the freeway. The visit to Mrs. Ford and the cemetery and then the quirky tarot card reading were not her typical Saturday activities. She hadn't had such a crazy day since high school, when she had dates with three different guys in an eight-hour period.

Her thoughts wandered back to the cemetery and the arrival of Ansel. She didn't understand how he could appear in a cemetery in another state but couldn't walk from the attic to the mailbox in front of her house. Perhaps being outside Texas made a difference. He'd asked if he could help her, but he had made it clear he couldn't do anything to erase the curse. She wondered about the falling-in-love resolution to end the curse. Did that mean he had to fall in love or someone had to fall in love with him?

And then, of course, there was the tarot card reading. How weird was that? Zoe flipped channels using the remote looking for a cable news channel, Fox or CNN. It was a few minutes past ten o'clock, so news should be on somewhere. Bingo, Fox News flickered around the darkened hotel room.

Zoe's mind rambled after hearing the second story on bombings in the Middle East. She thought back to Royal Street and Madam Larue. Although she knew tarot card readings were loony, fifteen bucks was a small price to hear she'd be the new owner of Merlin's. Rather than hearing that, the reading went in an unexpected and freaky direction that almost threw Zoe off the chair. Madam Larue's cards "predicted" she would marry a man whose initials were A.D.

What the hell did that mean? A.D. as in Ansel Delaney or Adam Dumbutt? Madame Larue acted like the initials were a clue—a clue to the curse or a clue that tarot readings entertained only and shouldn't be taken seriously. But, of all the initials in the world, why had she conjured the initials A.D.?

Zoe's eyelids drooped. She didn't have the energy to further evaluate the day. She snuggled into the pillows, reminding herself to think about the "clue" in the morning. Something brushed over her hair, and she raised her head from the pillow.

"Hello, darling. Did you have a good day?"

"Ansel, what the hell are you doing here?" Zoe looked first at her flannel pajamas and then at the spirit lounging at the end of her bed. "Don't call me 'darling.'"

"Oh, sweetie pie, don't be mad at me for dropping by. I miss you not being at home."

"Home? You mean my house?"

"Of course, sweetheart." He spread out on the bed, propping his head with a hand. "I was daydreaming earlier. I think you should quit your job and forget about buying Merlin's."

"What?" Zoe starred at his grinning face. "Not only are you dead, but you're dumb as a doorknob."

He sat up. "No need to get snippy."

"Sorry, poor choice of words," she said. "But think about it. How would I support myself without a job?"

"No problem."

"Perhaps from your point of view, not mine. I need to work to eat."

"No, you don't need to work. I'll support you. I have considerable assets."

"Yeah, right, and I'm first in line for the throne in Great Britain." She leaned toward Ansel and whispered, "Let me offer you a news flash. Ghosts don't have assets."

"I surmise you're much too tired to have a suitable conversation. I'll leave now." Ansel untangled himself from the bed and stood at its foot. "Nighty-night, I'll see you at home."

Chapter Eight

Zoe and Aunt Tina walked out of the hotel early on Sunday morning and headed to Café du Monde for coffee and beignets. As they strolled down Decatur Street, Zoe had a hard time shaking off the memory of last night's visit from Ansel. Not only was he the focus of her journey to New Orleans but he made sure she didn't forget it, or he was just being friendly.

Over steaming mugs of deep-roast chicory coffee and a plate of beignets dusted with powdered sugar, they considered the remainder of their agenda.

"Our plane leaves at three o'clock. What do you have planned until we leave for the airport? I assume it's not drinking coffee all day." Aunt Tina bit into a beignet and closed her eyes. "These are so good."

"I know." Zoe also munched on a beignet. "We have an appointment at eleven-thirty. I called earlier to confirm it."

"Who are we visiting?"

Zoe licked powdered sugar off the corner of her mouth. "I thought we might as well get the big picture while we're here."

"Uh-huh." Aunt Tina eyed a second beignet and snagged it off the plate.

"My research on Ansel's family revealed he has relatives living here as well."

"It seems strange that both Ansel and Charlotte have relatives in the same city outside of Houston. I hadn't realized there was such a strong New Orleans connection with his family."

"Neither had I."

Aunt Tina raised her coffee cup in salute. "As your mother and I have told you time and time again, family is the strongest bond of all."

"Absolutely." Zoe saluted her aunt as well. "That's why we're scheduled to visit Ruth Anne Simmons, who is a great-niece of Ansel Delaney II."

Tina looked stunned for a moment. "Ah, you're referring to Ansel's father. We are making the rounds here." She brushed sugar from her nose. "I do hope that sexy ghost of yours appreciates all the efforts on his behalf."

"I'm sure he does. But remember, the trip back to his grave means I'll be living alone in my house."

"I'll bet you a case of merlot you'll miss him."

"Maybe, I'm not sure." Zoe rose and brushed powdered sugar off her sleeve. "Let's do some window shopping on Royal Street. We have a couple of hours until our appointment."

They exited Café du Monde and walked across Decatur Street to Jackson Square. The park was about the size of a city block and bordered by a tall wrought iron fence. A statute of General Andrew Jackson sitting a horse graced the middle, with grass and flower beds completing the rest of the park. Street artists displayed paintings leaning against the fence as well as rickety tables laden with jewelry.

They soon walked around the corner of the square to the open area in front of St. Louis Cathedral. The space was filled with dark blue benches, a small jazz band playing for tourists, and several tables set up for either a tarot card or a psychic reading.

Aunt Tina touched Zoe's arm and nodded toward a tarot card reader behind a table with a yellow scarf over it, the ends fluttering in the morning breeze.

The female reader noticed the interaction and bellowed, "Come sit down with me. I'll tell you your dreams."

"Sorry, no time," Zoe said and leaned toward her aunt. "Come on, I don't need another reading. The one last night was enough."

They hiked over an uneven stone pathway bordering the side of the cathedral and soon came to Royal Street.

Aunt Tina looked left and right, looking perplexed. "You know I have no sense of direction. Which way?"

Zoe laughed and stabbed the air with an index finger. "Let's go left toward Canal Street."

They strolled along the sidewalk and occasionally walked in the narrow street, all the while enjoying the warmth of the sun. Street musicians played at the next corner, with a young boy tap dancing on the pavement. A crowd had formed around them and clapped in time to the country song. Zoe and Tina stopped to enjoy the music.

"This is why I love New Orleans," Aunt Tina whispered to Zoe. "Everyone is so spontaneous."

Zoe nodded and pulled a couple of bills out of her wallet and tossed them in the red donation can in the middle of the street. "They're very good, but we need to keep moving." She stepped back on the sidewalk, followed by her aunt. "There's a boutique a couple blocks down that I want to check out. I noticed it last night after dinner."

"Sounds good to me, you know I love shopping."

The traffic on the sidewalk was light, so they had an enjoyable time looking in the shop windows. Royal Street was a shopper's mecca. Zoe did drag Tina into one souvenir shop for chicory coffee and beignet mix for her mother and decided to treat herself as well. *I wonder if Ansel likes chicory coffee*. Damn it, she'd caught herself thinking about her ghost as though he eagerly waited for her at home and was human. Geez, she was confused.

They continued to window shop until they came upon the boutique, Your Destiny.

"Do you mind if we go in?" Zoe said.

"You go ahead. I'm going to that dress shop across the street. I'll be back in a couple of minutes."

"Okay, I'll meet you here." Zoe watched her aunt hurry across the street and then entered the boutique.

A bell jingled when she pushed on the scratched wooden door. She stepped inside, and the scent of sandalwood floated around her. She browsed the eclectic mix of souvenir items, original jewelry, magical charms, and one-of-a-kind handbags. *What a crazy mix of merchandise.*

She ambled along the counters and shelves, studying the stock with the eye of an experienced boutique shopper. She didn't see anything she couldn't live without. A purse caught her attention, but she had just bought a new one and couldn't rationalize spending the money. A display of magical charms and a basket with a hand-printed sign "Irish Wishing Stones" caught her attention. She picked up a small transparent bag of three stones, intrigued by their heaviness in her palm. Each stone was less than an inch in diameter and marbled in multiple shades of blue, grass green, and cream.

Zoe closed her fingers around the stones and was surprised at their warmth. That seemed odd. Because they were Irish stones, she decided to buy a bag. Ansel might know about them since he had an Irish background. That pleased and distressed her at the same time. He would be leaving soon, and it was a mistake to depend on him for anything.

∞

After checking out of the hotel, they retrieved the rental car from the valet and were soon looking at street signs in the Garden District.

"Zoe, what was that street name again?"

"Rue Violet. It has to be around here somewhere. Check the map again."

"You know map reading isn't one of my strong points." Nevertheless, Aunt Tina studied the map on her lap. She looked out the car window. "Wait, turn right at the next street. It should be the next street we cross."

Zoe followed her aunt's instructions, and sure enough, Rue Violet was next.

"Okay, Auntie, left or right?"

"I'm not sure," Aunt Tina answered. "Oh, what the hell, turn left. What's the street number we're looking for?"

"It's 121."

"Stop," Aunt Tina commanded. "There it is on the right."

Zoe slammed on the brakes, looked in the rearview mirror. Thankfully, a car wasn't behind them, or they might have had a collision. She took a deep breath and reminded herself to relax. Everything would work out just fine.

The door to an impressive red-brick two-story home opened before Zoe pushed the doorbell. A near-perfect clone of Sarah Ford stood in the doorway.

The woman spoke first. "Zoe Miller, I presume."

Zoe nodded, "This is my aunt, Tina Peters."

"Wonderful. I'm Ruthie Simmons. Please come in." She stepped aside, allowing Zoe and Tina to enter the foyer. It was smaller than the Ford house, but impressive nonetheless with matching five-foot crystal vases of orange mums on opposite sides of the entrance. Mrs. Simmons closed the door and crossed the foyer to a living room. Zoe and Aunt Tina trailed behind her.

Zoe had an intense sense of déjà vu once they settled on cream-colored sofas. She wondered if a standard decorating style populated New Orleans homes for the well-to-do.

"May I offer you coffee?" Mrs. Simmons asked.

"No, thank you." Aunt Tina replied.

"How may I help you?" Mrs. Simmons addressed Zoe. "You were rather vague on the phone. Something about my dear departed cousin, Ansel Delaney III, I believe you said. His spirit resides in the attic of your home?"

"Yes, that's correct." Zoe again considered how much to reveal to Ansel's relative. Every time she discussed him, she sank farther into his rabbit hole. "I know my call on Friday was out of the blue and no doubt sounded strange."

"Yes, strange." Mrs. Simmons nodded, smiling primly. "Intriguing as well. Since his death, Ansel the third has been a celebrity of sorts in the family."

"Really?" Aunt Tina raised her eyebrows.

"Interesting that the Delaney's would . . ." Zoe trailed off and wondered aloud, "What sort of celebrity?"

"I guess you'd call it the rock star kind," Mrs. Simmons said. "Even though most of the family had never met him, cousin Ansel has been the subject of many discussions over the years."

"Really?" Aunt Tina asked again. Zoe assumed she'd had too much sugar and patted her hand in reassurance.

"Mrs. Simmons, did the Delaney family talks revolve around one topic or another?"

"Why, yes," she replied. "His murder. Almost everyone had a theory about who murdered him and why."

Zoe sat straighter. Did she hear what she thought she'd heard. "The family had differing opinions about why he was killed?"

"Yes. They were all quite different." Mrs. Simmons lowered her voice and leaned forward. "I don't like to talk about this, but I will to help you and to help poor Ansel's spirit."

"We do appreciate that. What was the opinion of the Delaney family about the reason for his murder?" Zoe asked.

"His mother thought he got mixed up with the wrong people, probably politically related. She seemed certain he had angered someone powerful enough to put a contract on his life."

Aunt Tina grimaced. "That sounds terrible."

"Perhaps. Others questioned Maxim's motive, as Ansel had an affair with Maxim's longtime girlfriend, who became pregnant with his child. And Maxim had always been jealous of his older brother."

"My heavens, this sounds like a soap opera," Zoe exclaimed. "Was there any consensus as to who killed him?"

"Unfortunately, no. It seems as though everyone had their own theories." Mrs. Simmons clasped her hands in her lap. "The gossip I find the most disturbing involves Ansel's stepfather."

"William Whitmire," Zoe said. She had never discussed him with Ansel. "Did the two of them get along?"

"I overheard my parents talking about them. The gist was that they were polite face-to-face, but Ansel and William couldn't stand the sight of each other."

"I bet Ansel didn't like him marrying his mother," Aunt Tina offered. "I've heard sons can be protective and jealous of a mother's suitors."

"My guess is it was more than that," Mrs. Simmons confided. "I've always thought it related to the family business. Ansel didn't want him involved, and William kept butting in."

"I suppose both Maxim and William Whitmire wouldn't have been heartbroken after Ansel's murder," Zoe concluded. She turned to Aunt Tina. "I believe we have extra research to do. You may have to call your friend at the library."

Aunt Tina grinned. "No problem."

Mrs. Simmons looked at her watch. "My granddaughter will be here to pick me up for lunch. Are there any other questions?" She glanced from Tina to Zoe.

Zoe weighed her final question. Was it too blunt or simply too nosy? Oh, what the hell.

"I have one more," she said.

Mrs. Simmons rose and headed for the foyer. Zoe and Tina followed. With a hand on the doorknob, she turned to them. "Yes, Miss Miller, what is your last question?"

"Who do you think killed Ansel?"

Mrs. Simmons opened the door. She smiled gently and offered her hand. "I think you already know the answer to that. Have a good flight back to Houston."

Zoe drove on autopilot from Bush airport to her house. The flight back from New Orleans had been boring but thankfully quick. Her mind had been on overload. She distracted herself from thoughts about Ansel and what she had learned about his family by reading the in-flight magazine. It didn't work. Each time she turned a page, a picture popped into her head of Ansel or one of his ancestors. And she had no damned idea who killed him, regardless of Mrs. Simmons's certainty that she did.

Why did she constantly think about Ansel and his problems? Ridiculous. Ghosts didn't have problems. They were dead, for God's sake.

Zoe almost missed her exit off the freeway. Without a signal, she swung across two lanes of traffic and garnered minor road rage, expressed through blaring horns. She made a quick decision to go directly to parent's house rather than stopping at home first. Twenty minutes later she parked in their driveway, eager to see them after their month-long vacation.

Hopefully, the dinner wouldn't take too long. Zoe enjoyed family occasions, but today she was pooped and looked forward to climbing into her own bed. The two days in Louisiana seemed like a week.

"Hey, Mama." Zoe hugged her mother in the kitchen of her parent's Memorial area home and smelled the Chanel Mom always wore. Zoe would never tire of the sanctuary and safety her mother represented.

"Oh, baby, it's so good to see you."

"I'm glad you guys are home." Zoe moved to the counter housing several bottles of wine. She selected a bottle, expertly opened it, and poured a glass. "Mom?" Toni Miller nodded, so Zoe poured a second glass.

"Where's Dad?" Zoe asked.

"Where else? He's checking out the grill."

Zoe sipped her wine. "Now, give me all the details of your trip."

Toni launched into a quick summary of the vacation. Zoe assumed her father would provide the same descriptions of the sights. They were the epitome of two peas in a pod.

The door to the patio banged. Zoe's father entered the kitchen and made a beeline for her.

"Hey, baby." David Miller kissed the top of her head. "Good to see you. Anything new while we were gone?"

"I'm glad you're both home, for starters," she said and then grinned. "I'm old enough to admit I miss you when you're gone."

Toni gave her daughter a second hug. "We think it's nice you're old enough, too."

"Finally, we agree on something." Zoe sat on a leather stool along one side of the center island. "Actually, I do have two pieces of news, one lousy and one interesting."

"Always start with bad news so you can end on a high note."

They all turned. Aunt Tina, who stood in the doorway of the kitchen's back entrance to the kitchen, had her arms open. "I've missed you two."

After a few minutes of catching up, Tina urged Zoe to continue with her news.

"Mom, I told you yesterday the truly lousy news is that Mr. Allen has a second offer for Merlin's. Now I have competition."

"When will you hear his decision?" David asked while pouring a glass of wine for Tina.

"I hope by midweek," Zoe replied with a shrug. "My fingers are crossed that Mr. Allen will choose my offer."

"Hang in there, sweetheart." Toni patted Zoe's

arm on her way to check the oven. "Okay, we've heard the bad news. What's the interesting news?"

"She has quite the story to tell," Tina chimed in.

Zoe opened her mouth and shut it. How should she tell them she'd been canoodling with a ghost?

"You may think I'm nuts, but I've been talking with the ghost in the attic of Nana's house." There she'd said it. She'd explained her weirdest and most funny-farm-certifiable experience to her parents. The two people in the world she wanted to make proud. The two people in the world who could deflate her bubble of joy in an instant. The two people she no longer wanted to disappoint as she had so many times in the past.

She looked first at her father and then her mother. "Please, tell me. Am I nuts or what?"

"Sweetie, I must admit that Tina did give us a warning on this ghost issue," Toni said. "And no, we don't think you're nuts. Overtired, maybe?"

Munching on a carrot, David added, "I bet you've been worrying nonstop over the deal for Merlin's."

"Of course I'm worried." Zoe halfheartedly pounded on the counter with her fist. "I want to own the store." She noticed the surprised look on her parents' faces. "Sorry, guess I'm a little anxious."

After accepting a glass of wine from David, Tina kissed Zoe's cheek. "I suppose if you don't become a business owner there's that other alternative."

"What other alternative?" Toni asked.

"The one related to marrying A.D," Aunt Tina replied.

"What?" David and Toni voiced together.

∾

Zoe hummed along with the radio, looking forward to parking her suitcase and climbing into bed. She didn't want to think about Merlin's or the trip to New Orleans. She'd had a long two days and wanted a minimum of eight hours of downtime, minus serious thinking or problems on the horizon. Twenty minutes after leaving her parents' house, she parked in her driveway, grabbed her bag from the trunk, and climbed the front steps of her porch.

"That's weird. The living room lights are on." She moved her hand toward the door's lock and noticed the door was ajar. "What?" She pushed it open with her foot. "What's going on?"

Her eyes widened as she took in the disorder in her living room. She walked to the center and turned a full circle, trying to mentally process the mess around her. Cushions were off the sofa and chair, the bookshelf was empty, with books scattered on the rug, and the entertainment center was a confused mixture of wires. CD's normally stored on its shelves decorated the floor with squares of color.

She stumbled into the kitchen, as the lights were on there as well. Every cabinet door and drawer was open. The tile floor was littered with plastic wrap, paper napkins, silverware, and cooking utensils. The cabinet contents remained intact, yet still, this was another colossal mess.

"What the hell? Who did this?" Zoe grabbed the phone, dialed 911, and provided the details to the dispatcher.

She made her way upstairs and found a similar

mess in every room. Within five minutes she heard sirens on the street. Her stomach was in turmoil, and she wondered what was next.

The police left hours later, and her house was a further disaster. They didn't have any answers to why her home had been ransacked but assured her they'd be in touch.

She didn't have the energy to clean up the mess. She locked all the doors and trudged up the stairs to her bedroom, dragging the suitcase behind her. She changed into pajamas and climbed into her bed. Both the coolness of the sheets and the comforting sense of being at home began to relax her body and her mind. Yet, she struggled to unwind with the quiet in the room.

Her thoughts turned to the last two days and the string of weird events. First, she was almost run off the road after arriving in New Orleans. Second, Mrs. Ford explained that Ansel's mother had placed the curse on him with an Irish wishing stone. And third, Mrs. Simmons assumed Zoe had already figured out the identity of Ansel's killer. Finally, her home was broken into while she was away. Her life had taken a strange turn from party girl to ghost hunter. What was next?

Chapter Nine

Something stabbed at Zoe's foot. She kicked at it. A tactile sizzle inched up her ankle.

"What the hell?" She threw back the covers and lurched up.

"Hey, gorgeous, how was your trip?"

"Ansel, please, I need my sleep."

He stood at the foot of her bed, blue eyes crinkling, and unfortunately, he was chuckling. "Wake up, sleepyhead."

"What's with you? Go away." Zoe squinted at the clock: six a.m., much too early considering the last two days. She snuggled back into the sheets and closed her eyes.

A screeching train whistle spiraled through the bedroom. Zoe rolled over, hands over her ears.

"Stop it," she spit out. "Please let me sleep."

"No can do." He sat on the edge of the bed. "I want to hear all about your trip to New Orleans. I have a hunch it'll be enlightening."

"You're not going to leave me alone, are you?"

"Nope."

"I need coffee." Why argue with him? "I'll meet you in the kitchen. We need to talk about the break-in anyway." She swung her legs over the side of the bed while Ansel stayed rooted at the end. "I need some privacy here."

"Right, I'll wait for you downstairs." He evaporated with the snap of his fingers.

Zoe strolled into the kitchen intending to brew her coffee—not necessary. The aroma of Sumatra Roast filled the air. And the mess she came home to in the living room, as well as the kitchen, had disappeared. "How did this happen?"

"I think you set the pot last night," Ansel replied. He leaned against the sink.

"I don't remember that, but whatever." She pulled a cup from a cabinet, gave him a brilliant smile, and poured and savored the first jolt of caffeine. "This is almost worth getting up so early." She turned to him. "I assume you're responsible for cleaning up the mess from the break-in. Thank you. I don't understand how you can accomplish that, but thank you nonetheless. By the way, did they get in the attic? Did you see who trashed my house?"

"Nope, they didn't get in. The door was locked, and they couldn't break it down. I'm sure it's scratched though."

"Do all ghosts have magical powers?"

"How would I know?" He shrugged and winked at her. "I don't know any ghosts, other than me."

"Sure seems strange that you've suddenly taken an interest in this house."

"I guess your charm won me over," Ansel said.

"Sure, right. Back to the question of the day—why did you wake me up so early?"

"It's not early. It's the normal time you get up for work."

"Whatever," she said and shrugged. "I had planned on sleeping in and being late to work." She slugged down more coffee.

"I had hoped we could talk before you leave." He revealed the pathetic look. "I get so lonely by myself."

"Knock it off. Your pitiful face won't work today." Zoe laughed over her cup. He was cute without even trying. "I assume you want to know about my visit to New Orleans."

He bowed to her and sat at the bistro table. "Please tell me about your trip, step by step. You know, in chronological order."

Zoe raised her eyebrows, chronological order? This guy, uh, ghost was a tad on the anal side. Had he been an accountant when he was alive?

"No, Zoe. I wasn't a bean counter."

"Geez, can you read minds with all your other talents?"

"Sort of," he said, grinning like a dime-store clown. "Now, tell me about New Orleans."

"Fine. We'll talk about you later." She sat at the table. "The flight was fine. We were almost hit by an SUV as we left the rental car lot at the airport."

"Louisiana has lousy drivers?"

"Don't know. I think it was intentional."

"What? Were you—"

Zoe raised a hand to stop Ansel's questions. "Please, hear me out." He nodded, and she went on. "I think the near accident was intentional because once we were on the interstate, an identical or the same vehicle tried to run us off the road."

Ansel rose. "Why didn't you tell me about this at the cemetery?"

Zoe waved a hand at him and rose. "I tried to shake him off for several minutes. He finally drove off once we stopped along the shoulder and a police car pulled up. We didn't see the SUV for the rest of our trip."

"Maybe it was a bad joke by some nut who doesn't like rental cars."

"I don't think so." Zoe poured more coffee and returned to the table.

"Let's assume it was planned. That means it must have been a warning of some sort."

"Absolutely," she agreed. "Someone didn't want us in New Orleans asking questions."

"Didn't I warn you about that?" Her only response was a halfhearted shrug, so Ansel continued. "Who knew you were going there?"

"Jill and Mr. Allen since I decided on the trip at Merlin's. My parents and Aunt Tina probably told Teddy Ward."

"The people you visited in New Orleans could have told anyone."

Zoe snapped her fingers. "That's it. You're right. Someone in the Delaney, Whitmire or Dodd families doesn't want me asking questions." She gazed into Ansel's blue eyes and waved a finger at him. "They aren't fond of questions about you and your murder."

❧

Zoe arrived at work only one hour late. A mini miracle since she and Ansel had talked for almost an hour. She'd recited the conversations with both Sara Dodd and Mrs. Simmons with as much detail as she could remember. He seemed surprised by how much she had learned about his family and promised to spend the day sorting out the details with his seventy-year-old memory.

Once she walked into her office, she thanked her good luck for arriving when she did. Merlin's was besieged by over a dozen boxes of Christmas inventory. It was her job to sort them out and begin planning the holiday displays. A job that kept her mind occupied and off the subject of Ansel Delaney for hours.

Mr. Allen poked his head into the back office early afternoon, telling her it would only be a couple more days before he'd announce his decision. Her stomach rolled. Considering the craziness in her life lately, she figured she should develop a Plan B, even though she didn't want to. Purchasing Merlin's was all she wanted to focus on. Tears welled in her eyes, and she brushed them away with a shaky swipe of her fingertips. She had to be practical and consider the worst might happen, and she'd lose Merlin's.

The problem was that she couldn't think of another alternative for earning a paycheck. Sure, she could freelance some magazine articles, but it would take years to build a large enough network of editors to make a steady living. One job she sure as hell wouldn't do was working at a bank—unless she was beyond desperate. Just the thought of it gave her the jitters.

She took a deep breath and rubbed her hands together, closing her eyes. "Somehow, someway,

Merlin's will work out for me. I have to keep my faith and think only positive thoughts." Her eyes opened and lovingly glanced at the mess of books and boxes scattered on the floor. "Keep the faith, Zoe. Everything will be just fine."

Aunt Tina called midafternoon, providing a welcome relief from verifying the packing slip in every box of books.

"Sweet pea, how are you today?"

"I'm fine, a little tired. I woke up way too early this morning," Zoe said.

"Too much on your mind?"

"No. Ansel decided he just had to hear about our weekend and woke me up."

"He goes in your bedroom?"

"It's more like he simply appears without an invitation. Forget that, what's up?"

"Teddy and I were talking about the weekend over breakfast."

"Over breakfast?" Aunt Tina had once again surprised Zoe.

"Don't be provincial. I explained to him the gist of our visits to Mrs. Ford and Mrs. Simmons. I also told him about that crazy SUV."

"Surely you didn't tell him about the tarot card reading."

"Of course not. He thinks someone in one of the families doesn't like you asking questions about your ghost. Don't forget his murder was never solved."

"Ansel and I came to the same conclusion," Zoe said. "The next step is more research on the three families."

"Teddy is going to help with that. He's drawing up family trees for births after 1900."

"Excellent. That will give us a clear picture of the players. Thanks, Auntie. By the way, anything special going on between you and Teddy?"

"Maybe . . . perhaps, possibly."

Zoe laughed. "That's a definite yes."

∾◡∾

Sam Dodd called that evening as Zoe loaded the dishwasher. "Hi, what's up?"

"Are you free for dinner tomorrow evening? I was thinking Mexican or a steak."

"It just so happens that I am free." Zoe sat on the kitchen stool. "Mexican sounds fantastic."

"You read my mind. I'll pick you up at seven."

"Perfect." Zoe danced around the kitchen. Sam was the perfect antidote to neutralize her problems. He looked like an underwear model and acted like a gentleman. The ideal man to kick start her new attitude on life. Once she had Ansel and his curse resolved, she'd be free of problems and have more time to devote to her love life. But for now, a dinner date was a great start.

After Sam's call, Zoe climbed the stairs to her study, intending to work on the magazine article. She opened the document file on her computer and reread the opening.

"Not bad. Where do I go with this article?" She stared at the computer monitor for several moments. With the outline from last week forgotten, she began to type.

No doubt every case of a resident spirit is as individual as the human side of the spirit. Thus, homeowner must assess their ghosts without preconceived notions of the spirit world. First, don't allow stereotypes to sway one's thinking. Do not think of the spirit as the happy cartoon character, Casper the Ghost.

Each one is different, and few stationed in a home are truly happy. How could they be? They're dead and in an intermediary state between life and burial. And second, realize the ghost is most likely dealing with an unresolved issue from his or her human life. The homeowner who desires to rid a home of the live-in guest must resolve the issue causing the intermediary state.

Let me illuminate a few details about my own situation—

"Having fun?"

Zoe jumped in the chair and turned toward the voice. Ansel sat in the ratty old wicker chair in the corner. He looked as fresh as a casket rose.

"Nana loved that chair you're in," Zoe commented. He raised his eyebrows. Zoe frowned. "She had it on the patio and drank her first cup of coffee in it every morning. She enjoyed rituals like that."

"I remember. Your grandmother was a special woman."

"That she was. I'll always miss her." Zoe sighed. "I like to think she would approve of my plans for the patio and backyard."

"Are they firmed up yet?" Ansel asked.

"I have some ideas, but what I eventually do depends on how much money I have to spend. That reminds me, I'm working on the magazine article again."

"Guess it takes your mind off everything else going on."

"Yep," Zoe said. "I'm keeping my fingers crossed."

"I'm curious. Why is it so important that you own Merlin's?"

"It's a long story. The short version is that I was a very irresponsible teenager. I gave my parents way too much grief for no reason other than being spoiled."

"You're not the only one," Ansel said.

"I finally got my act together in college, thanks to an English professor. Owning a business will ensure I'll be able to support myself and . . ." Her voice quivered as she spoke. "Make my parents proud of me rather than creating problems they have to deal with."

"Sounds admirable. But what are your plans if Mr. Allen doesn't accept your offer? Will you continue to work at the bookstore?" Ansel naturally asked a logical question.

"Good questions but no Plan B. I don't have a clue as to what I'll do. I realize I need to seriously think about it. Right now, I'm procrastinating. I'd rather be optimistic and assume things will go my way."

"Good enthusiasm."

"What work did you do?" Zoe asked before she qualified her query. "When you were alive, that is."

"I was the president of a manufacturing

company."

Zoe's mouth fell. "Weren't you a little young for a job like that?"

"I didn't think so at the time. It was a family business." His eyes clouded a bit as he continued. "I took the job when my father died."

"Did your family accept you being the new boss?"

He looked surprised. "I never heard any complaints. But now, I wonder if someone didn't like it." He said through thin lips, "Someone who was willing to murder to get me out of the way."

"You've never thought about this before?"

"No. What could I do to uncover the identity of the murderer?"

"You might be surprised." She had a hunch Ansel had more power than even he imagined.

❧

Once Zoe backed out of the driveway the next morning, Ansel made a beeline for her study. He had an idea that involved her computer. He said a quick prayer and lowered himself into the chair in front of the desk. Nothing exploded, no smoke—so far, so good.

He'd witnessed Zoe turn on the computer by punching the On button dozens of times. Yet for a ghost, this simple act required extraordinary mental concentration. Hmm, it shouldn't be too difficult. After all, he could work a television with a remote control and load a coffee pot now. His arm reached toward the computer's operating unit, and his index finger zeroed in on the button. He squeezed his eyes shut and pressed the end of his finger against the button.

Something hummed. His eyes opened to the wonderful sight of the monitor coming to life.

"Damn, I'm good." Once all the little jumpy things stopped moving, he leaned in close to the screen to study their shapes. One of the doodads was the access to the Internet. Many times he'd watched Zoe use the hand thing she called a mouse—such a silly name for the glob of plastic—by moving it around and then pressing on it with her index finger. That sounded easy.

After thirty minutes of trial and error and a good dose of swearing, Ansel had mastered clicking with the mouse and was able to open Zoe's online Internet software. His head hurt, but he ignored it. Next was doing a search, as she called hunting for stuff.

Zoe always typed words into the long rectangle and then clicked on the orange box that said Web Search. He would do the same. He wanted to learn about his family's company, so he'd start with the name. Again using his index finger, he hit the letter keys one after the other: J-&-L-M-A-N-U-F-A-C-T-U-R-I-N-G. He clicked on the search box without straining his finger. *Ha ha.*

Whoa, all kinds of things appeared. He knew they were called links because they were in lines of words in blue. Another thing Zoe had told him.

Next was the hard part—deciding on the blue line that would provide the most information. Well, hell, he'd mimic Zoe once again and look at each link. He had all day to do his research. Damn, that sounded good, doing research. Ansel beamed, so proud of himself for figuring out how to help Zoe. He concentrated and clicked on the first link. The screen filled with a newspaper article.

Holy smokes, what in the world? He peered closer to the screen and read a few lines of the story about Bobby Delaney Jr. Damn it, this was unacceptable and beneath a Delaney.

∽

Zoe arrived at Merlin's a few minutes early and started a pot of coffee. Slowly returning to the back office through the center aisle, she took a deep breath. The store smelled magnificent—dusty and earthy, vanilla from the potpourri bowl on the front desk, and the musky aroma of ink on a page. Zoe loved the smell. It was in her blood and caressed every pore of her body. She loved books, and she loved working in a bookstore. No matter the outcome with Mr. Allen, she would continue to work in some capacity with books. Bookstore owner or employee or perhaps even author, it didn't matter. A smile graced her face, perhaps she had a Plan B after all.

She became engrossed in reviewing the Christmas inventory from the previous day. After an hour, Jill carried in a cup of coffee.

"Thanks. I forgot all about it," Zoe said.

"No problem. You're so quiet back here, everything okay?"

"Concentrating on the numbers. You know how I love to count books," Zoe said.

"What can I do to help?"

"I'm about done checking in the inventory. You can help me figure out the displays."

"I like working on them. Let me know when

you're ready, and I'll get the sketch pad."

After another hour or so, Zoe finished her two-day task. Every box had been examined, and nothing was out of order. A good omen.

Aunt Tina called around eleven o'clock saying Teddy would have the family trees ready by the end of the day, and she would fetch them from him at dinner that evening. They made a date to meet for breakfast Wednesday morning. Zoe hadn't yet worked through and analyzed all that she had learned in New Orleans. Knowing all the players would help her to organize her thoughts. During college, she had routinely used charts and other graphics to help with her studies. Once she got serious about them, that is, post-party-girl days.

∿

Zoe dabbed Chanel behind her ears and checked her image in the mirror. Not bad. She still needed new highlights and a haircut. She'd dressed nice casual with a slinky red sweater over her favorite date jeans. Bill had told her more than once they made her butt look good.

The doorbell rang just as she hit the bottom of the stairs. She opened the front door to a smiling and sexy-as-hell Sam.

He kissed her on the cheek. "You look great. Ready?"

After gathering her purse and keys, she locked the door. Sam followed her to his car. "Nice jeans."

At Escalante's, a popular Mexican restaurant in the trendy Highland Village area, Sam ordered Cuervo Gold margaritas with made-at-the table guacamole.

He clinked his glass against Zoe's. "Here's to a

great dinner. How was your weekend?"

"Good. My aunt and I flew to New Orleans."

"To enjoy Bourbon Street?"

"No. I had to do some research for an article I'm writing, and she decided to tag along." Zoe debated whether she should tell him the article centered on a ghost stuck in her attic. Nope, better not. She didn't know him well enough to judge how he might react. He'd probably think she was nuts talking about a ghost.

"I didn't know you were a writer," he commented with a sloppy smile. "What's the article about?"

"Girl stuff: clothes, makeup, shoes." She didn't enjoy bending the truth but now wasn't the time not to bend it.

"Sounds interesting, I guess." He laughed and their food arrived.

Over dinner, Zoe mentioned the break-in at her house.

Sam's eyes widened. "That's horrible. Was anything taken? Are you all right?"

"Yes, I'm fine. Nothing is missing. They just made a huge mess."

"I'm sorry you've had to deal with that. Did they tear up your entire house?" Sam queried with sympathy in his voice.

"Even the garage had some damage. But the only room they didn't get into was the attic."

"The attic, huh?" Sam moved his gaze from his plate to Zoe. "Why is that? Superman lock?"

Zoe definitely couldn't tell him why. "Yeah, a good lock and a strong door." Ansel would laugh his head off if he knew she'd agreed he had the strength of Superman.

"That's good."

Zoe closed her eyes for a second, enjoying the spicy flavor of her spinach enchiladas. "You know what's funny? The only items in the attic are a rocking chair, a pile of junk that was my grandmother's, and that trunk of old books from Merlin's I mentioned to you before. Nothing of interest to a burglar."

Sam choked as he sipped his margarita.

"Are you okay?" Zoe asked.

"Too much salt."

The rest of the dinner included heavy doses of flirting, which Zoe thoroughly enjoyed. It had been much too long since she had batted her eyelashes and cocked her head to the right or the left at every clever remark by a handsome man. She even twirled her hair on a finger.

Sam escorted her to the front porch a few minutes after ten o'clock. Like a gentleman, he put the key in the door lock for her and pressed her against the door with his body. He cupped her head and firmly kissed her. Zoe had just enough time for a quick breath before he again captured her lips and deepened the kiss. Her knees became weak, and she grabbed his arm to steady herself. Abruptly, he stepped back.

"It's getting late. I better go. I'll call you." Sam kissed Zoe on the cheek and then turned and hurried down the steps. He waved as he opened his car door.

She questioned his hasty departure. "Men are so weird!" Zoe stomped into the house, slamming the door behind her. "'I'll call you' from a guy means 'kiss off woman.'"

"Are you sure about that?"

Zoe skidded to a stop. Ansel lounged in the recliner with the TV remote in his hand.

"What are you doing in here?" she asked, throwing her purse and keys on the sofa.

"I live here," he said easily.

"No, you don't. You're trapped here." She shook her head. "It's an intermediary stop to your grave."

"Details. How was your date?"

"Fine, just dandy." She zeroed in on his hand. "How can you hold that remote?"

He looked at it, turned it in his hand. "Concentration."

"What?"

"Did you see the movie *Ghost*?"

"Who hasn't?"

"Good. Near the end, Patrick Swayze moves a penny up a door and puts it in Demi Moore's hand on the other side. Remember that scene?"

"I think so." Zoe's favorite scene was when the two characters were both behind the pottery wheel, their hands immersed in wet clay. That was one sexy scene.

"I can hold an object using the same technique." He tossed the remote in the air in front of his chest and caught it. "It's mental concentration in its purest form."

"You're playing with me."

"No. That's the way it works. I've been able to keep up with the changes in the world by watching television." He was silent a moment. "By the way, have you given any thought to buying a high-definition plasma TV, around fifty inches or more?"

"What?"

"Can't you just see *Monday Night Football* on a big screen?"

She didn't notice the crinkling of his eyes or his efforts to hold back a chuckle

"You are the most impossible person I've ever met." She started toward the stairs and turned back to him. He was so damned handsome and a nice guy—a truly dangerous combination. "I'm going to bed now, so please, do not wake me up in the morning."

"Good night, Zoe. I'll think about it."

Chapter Ten

Zoe gave her proper navy suit a second glance in the mirror. The pearls were too much, so she replaced them with a gold chain and a dangly pendant. Perfect.

Today was the day. She hoped the suit and heels would produce good, no great, business karma. Today she would finally learn her fate—whether or not owning Merlin's Favorite Bookstore was in her future. For good luck, she crossed her fingers and repeated "Today will be a great day" seven times.

Ansel waited for her in the kitchen, leaning against the counter in front of the window. She made a beeline for the coffeepot.

"Good morning, Ansel. You're up early."

"Good morning to you as well. You're looking businesslike today."

"That's the plan. I'm in a hurry, so I don't have time to talk." She poured coffee in her favorite travel mug and headed for the front door. She turned back to him. "Don't be buying any plasma TVs from the Home Shopping Network." Zoe giggled at Ansel's startled expression. "Have a good one."

Peeking out the front window, Ansel watched Zoe's car turn right at Dunlavy Street. "Best of luck, my love. I'll be right here waiting to hear the good news."

He quickly flashed to the rocking chair. The attic was cool due to the fall weather. For almost his entire tenure in the attic, he'd hated the cold weather seeping in through hairline cracks in the walls and around the windows. It slowed his reflexes. He rocked to warm his presence and his soul.

To be truthful, his spirits were lower than the sun at dusk. His plan to gain Zoe's trust and then her love had stalled before he'd had a chance to put it in motion. This Sam Dodd character reminded him of vinegar stirring into his chocolate cheesecake batter. But what could he do about the guy? Call him out to a duel? No, better yet, Ansel could challenge Sam to . . . What?

Damn it. The reality was he couldn't do anything to prevent Zoe's interest in Sam. Sam. Sam. He hated that name, always had. It reminded him of a bully kid from second grade who had made his life miserable the entire school year. It was one of those experiences a person couldn't shake off, memories taken to an almost grave.

He resigned himself to Sam being around. He'd simply have to work harder on Zoe. After all, she was the key to unlocking the curse.

∾

Zoe and Aunt Tina arrived at the Eggs Rock Bistro off Shepherd at the same time.

"Zoe, my heavens, you look so professional this morning." Aunt Tina kissed her cheek. "Love your suit."

"Thanks. It's my good luck charm."

They were ushered to a table by a sunny window. After placing their breakfast orders, Aunt Tina spread the family trees on the table.

"Teddy said he had fun doing these. As you know, he's a genealogy buff," Tina said.

Zoe looked at each oversized chart. She recognized many of the names but some were unfamiliar. "I have a feeling the answer to lifting the curse and discovering Ansel's murderer is on one of these charts. Maybe we have an Irish ancestor after all."

"Mama would be so proud. She had a touch of the gift."

"I've always been told she did, but I thought it was more gypsy related. But why couldn't she contact Ansel?"

"I think you should ask him that question."

The food arrived, and their coffee cups were refilled. Zoe thoroughly enjoyed her "good for your health" bananas and oatmeal.

She thought about her aunt's suggestion. "I have to figure this out on my own."

"Because he can't tell you anything?" Tina asked, a fork waving in the air.

"Yes, that's what I have to deal with." Zoe blinked and her eyes gleamed. "But Teddy gave us some good clues with the family trees."

"Where do we start?"

"I think we should begin with talking to whoever in the families is still alive here in Houston." Zoe glanced at the Delaney chart. "Like Robert Delaney Sr.

I'll check him out on the Internet."

"Good plan." Aunt Tina raised her coffee cup in salute. "Change of subject. When do you expect to hear from Mr. Allen?"

"Not sure, exactly, but it should be today."

"I do hope it turns out the right way, sweet pea."

"Me, too." Zoe crossed her fingers again for good luck.

~⁓

A few minutes after leaving Aunt Tina, Zoe unlocked the front door to Merlin's. The store was eerily quiet. She'd never before noticed the intensity of the silence when she was alone. The store was simply resting and gearing up for a busy day.

Zoe once again started the coffee and then hurried to her office. She tossed Teddy's charts on her desk and turned on the computer. The e-mail program booted up, so she checked her messages, nothing from Mr. Allen or his business broker. Nana always said no news was good news. She sure as hell hoped that was true today. It was too early to start a worry fest. She'd give it until four o'clock. If she hadn't heard from either of them by four, well, then she'd go ballistic. Until then, she had work to do.

For the next six hours, she did her best to keep her mind on her job. She reviewed book orders for Valentine's Day and worked with Jill on the Christmas displays. Once every fifteen minutes, she wondered about her offer for Merlin's, but quickly dropped the thought.

Unable to shake off her nerves, at three o'clock she took a walk around the block. The afternoon was sunny with clear skies and almost eighty degrees, typical south Texas weather for early October. She stopped at the ice cream store a couple of doors down from Merlin's and ordered a double mint-chocolate cone. A short while later, she strolled back to her office with her chocolate craving satisfied. She continued to hold her breath every time the phone rang.

Finally, a bit after four o'clock, she gave up the pretense of working. She sat at her desk and stared into space, at the phone, out the window. By four twenty, the paper clips in an old coffee mug numbered 232, and the top of her desk held five neat stacks of file folders and papers.

Jill poked her head around the door curtain. "Hey, there's a call for you on the main line."

"Thanks." Zoe squeezed her eyes followed by her fists. She counted to five before picking up the phone and punching the button for the correct line.

"This is Zoe Miller. How may I help you?"

Mr. Allen's business broker got right to the purpose of his call. "Miss Miller, a few minutes ago I finished a two-hour meeting with Jack Allen. We all reviewed our final evaluation of the two proposals to purchase the bookstore."

"Great." At last a decision had been made. Zoe tensed and held her breath.

"He gave each proposal equal consideration. In the end he has decided to accept the offer from the other party."

"What?" Zoe's breath came out in a rush as her stomach bounced off the floor. "He accepted the other offer?"

"That's correct. He'll be out of the store through the end of the week but plans to talk to you on Monday. He asked me to convey to you he hopes you'll continue your employment with Merlin's."

"I . . . I don't know." Her mind reeled, direction unknown.

"I know this is a letdown. Please give Mr. Allen's desire for your continued employment some thought. You never know what the future will bring. May I answer any questions for you?"

"No, no. I need to absorb all this. Thanks for calling." Zoe slowly replaced the receiver. She sank into the desk chair like a deflating latex balloon. Absently tapping a pencil on the desk, she once again stared out the window and questioned her own reality. How could this be happening to her? Her dreams, her future, her business plans had disappeared as quickly as a spring shower sprinkling the garden. And seriously, what new owner would want keep her on as an employee? How would she tell her parents?

Over an hour later, Jill appeared at the office door. "I'm going now. I've got a class in a few minutes."

Zoe didn't turn around and said on autopilot, "Go ahead. See you tomorrow."

"Everything okay?" Jill asked. "You sound strange."

Zoe felt the itch of Jill's eyes staring at her back. "I'm fine. Have a good class."

Thirty minutes later, a calmer Zoe packed her briefcase and declared it time to close the store. She shooed the other salesclerk out of the building and felt no guilt in ending the workday eight minutes early. Without thinking about her actions, she turned off the store's lights and locked the front door. Ten minutes later she pulled into her driveway without a single memory of how she arrived home so quickly.

∾

Zoe sat cross-legged in the middle of her living room sofa. A large bowl of pasta smothered in creamy alfredo sauce rested in her lap. A hunk of French bread with garlic and melted mozzarella was to her left, and a glass of merlot sat on a telephone book to her right. The bread and wine were within easy reach, along with the TV remote.

She clicked the remote and surfed her favorite movie channels. Luck rained down. *Sleepless in Seattle* had just started. It was one of her all-time favorite chick movies and guaranteed to take her mind off the day's rotten news.

Damn it! Life sucks. Stop. No thinking about that. She decided to bring back the wine bottle from the kitchen. It was a long movie.

Zoe heard whistling just as Jonah and his father spotted Meg Ryan walking towards them on the observation deck of the Empire State Building.

"Ansel, show yourself," she shouted.

The noise spiraled throughout the living room before it quieted down. Smoke appeared directly in front of the television.

"Move," Zoe commanded. "You're blocking my view."

The smoke dissipated. "Good evening to you as well." Ansel positioned himself in the recliner. His gaze inspected the sofa and the remnants of her dinner. "Enjoying the film?"

"What for?" she asked.

"Excuse me?" Ansel frowned.

"Go away," Zoe said and hiccupped. "You don't belong here."

"Are you feeling all right?"

She rescued the wine bottle from the floor, poured the last drop in her glass. She held it up in front of her chest, facing Ansel. "Here's to you, my friendly ghost. Now, go 'way. I don't want company."

"Have a bad day?"

"Well, gee, Ansel, whadya think? Did ya see me come home singin' and dancin'?"

"I surmise you received bad news related to Merlin's." He rose and stood before her, concern lighting his dark blue eyes.

"My, my, you're clairvo . . . clairyant. You know what I mean." Zoe emptied her glass, tossed it to the corner of the sofa cushions. She gazed at him, eyes glistening. "Course it was bad news. Pulleezze, go away. I don' wanna talk with you or anyone else."

He frowned again and then evaporated, followed by a single minuscule beam of light that momentarily blinked, then was dark.

"Good riddance, ya old ghost." Zoe hiccupped again and rose, swaying a bit before steadying herself. Her original plan to get another bottle of wine evaporated after she noticed the stairs. Resting for a few minutes on her soft bed seemed like a fine idea. She slowly made her way up each stair, careful to place a foot squarely on each step. She crawled into bed and promptly fell asleep. Eventually, Ansel filled her dreams with either wishful thinking or an overactive imagination.

The water was warm and the clearest of blues on the color wheel. Along the shoreline, Zoe could make out pebbles and shells lying on the ocean floor. She kicked the water as she strolled, enjoying its coolness as it splashed against her bare legs. The day was glorious. She didn't have a care in the world.

She studied the sun, analyzing its place in the morning sky. Ansel should be at the house by now. Eager to see him, she picked up her pace, moving out of the water to the soft white sand.

Within a couple of minutes, she approached the wooden stairs leading from the beach to the back deck of her parents' vacation home. She hurried up the first flight, paused to catch her breath at the landing, and then continued to climb another flight that opened to the patio. The patio hugged the back of the house on the main floor and circled the side to the master bedroom.

She ran to the sliding doors and poked her head in. "Ansel, are you here?" She waited a moment and repeated the question.

She smiled at the sight of him walking out of the bedroom. "There you are."

"I was in the closet."

If Zoe lived to two hundred, she would never lose the pleasure she experienced right at that moment when she watched him walk toward her. He had a swagger so masculine she could barely keep herself from falling at his feet and pledging her love and loyalty to the end of time.

He reached her and kissed her firmly on the lips. "Hi, babe, have a good walk?"

"It was wonderful. I swear the sand at Galveston beach is getting whiter each year."

"Must have something to do with global warming," he commented. "Do you want to change before we go to lunch?"

"Lunch?" Zoe asked.

"Remember? With your parents at the yacht club." He kissed her again and patted her butt. "Go get changed."

"I need to take a shower first." She kissed him back and pulled his hand, leading him to the bedroom. "Keep me company."

"My pleasure." He grinned wickedly and followed her.

She began to pull off clothes once she entered the room. The garments silently settled on the oak floor. Ansel followed suit behind her. She entered the bathroom and started the shower, testing the water with her hand.

He stood right behind her, a sparkle in his eye. His hands snaked around her waist and settled on her breasts.

"I'll gladly keep you company. Hop in."

She turned to face him, laughing, "I meant keep me company by talking with me. But," she sucked on his lower lip. "This is much better."

They entered the shower and turned to face each other. Ansel hugged her with intensity—

The bedside phone would not stop ringing. She

wanted to know what sexy thing Ansel would do with her, but the phone was too annoying. She grabbed it.

"What?"

"Is this Zoe Miller?"

She jerked up, her head not appreciating the quick movement. She didn't recognize the voice. Late night phone calls always gave her a fright. The digital clock read 4:51. "Yes, this is Zoe."

"This is Detective Joe Sanders with the Houston Police Department."

Her heart twisted into a knot.

"Your name is listed on the alarm permit for Merlin's Favorite Bookstore."

"Yes, my name is there as well as the owner, Mr. Allen. Is there a problem?"

"The bookstore was burglarized late last night or early this morning."

"Didn't the alarm scare them off?"

"It appears the alarm wasn't set," the detective answered. "Mr. Allen is with me at the store. Would you mind coming down? I can have a patrol car pick you up."

"Of course, yes, I'll be right there." Zoe jumped out of bed, stumbling over her shoes. She righted herself. "A car isn't necessary. I'm just a few minutes away, so I'll drive myself."

"Good, we'll see you shortly." The detective clicked off.

She replaced the phone and sat on the bed, tears running down her cheeks. She knew in her heart she was responsible for the burglary. She closed the store last night, so she was the one who hadn't set the alarm.

Would the police assume she had done it on purpose?

~~

After a quick shower and a good teeth brushing with ample mouthwash, Zoe set off for the bookstore. For once, she drove at the speed limit. She turned right at Kirby Drive and pulled behind a patrol car along the curb. She spied Mr. Allen talking with a uniformed police officer just inside the main door. All the store's lights were on, illuminating its front and the sidewalk.

She stepped up to the walk, and Mr. Allen pointed in her direction. A man exited the front door and approached her.

"Miss Miller?"

"Are you Detective Sanders?"

"I need to talk with you before you see Mr. Allen." He gestured to a metal bench a few feet away. They settled on the cold seat, a wide space between them. "Miss Miller, I understand you closed the store yesterday evening." His eyes focused on the sidewalk. "You also learned that same day that your offer to purchase Merlin's wasn't accepted by Mr. Allen."

"That's true, but it doesn't—"

"Please, just answer my question." Detective Sanders looked at her and offered a grim smile. "What was your reaction to Mr. Allen's decision?"

"I was shocked, surprised. All along I had expected him to accept my offer. The second party that became involved at the end of the negotiations was a huge surprise to me."

"Do you hold a grudge because of it?"

"Absolutely not." She would never have bitterness against Mr. Allen.

"Fine." He jotted on a small notebook he'd taken from his coat pocket. "What time did the store close last night?"

"A few minutes before six."

"Why early?"

"I was upset, and there weren't any customers." Zoe realized she needed to be clear on this point. "A few minutes wasn't going to hurt anyone."

"Tell me exactly what you did." The detective held his notebook, ready for note taking.

"An hour and a half after talking with the business broker, I wanted to go home, to put the bad news behind me. Since it was my turn to close the store, I decided to close up early. I told the clerk to go home, gathered my briefcase, turned off the lights, and left through the front door. I locked the door after I was on the sidewalk."

"You don't remember turning on the alarm?"

"No."

"Was it intentional?"

"Heavens, no." Zoe couldn't believe someone would think she had failed to set the alarm on purpose. But she had to admit it did seem logical under the circumstances. "By the way, how was the break-in discovered?"

"A patrol car making its rounds noticed the open front door around three a.m." He rose from the bench. "You can see Mr. Allen now. I'll have more questions later."

"No problem, detective. I'll go see Mr. Allen now."

She took a deep breath to calm her nerves and

walked into the store, eyes searching for Mr. Allen. She found him near the coffee bar, checking supplies.

"Hi, Mr. Allen," she said carefully. He looked at her then turned back to the packets of sugar. "I hope you know I feel terrible about this. It's an accident that I didn't set the alarm last night."

"I don't know what to believe. But I'm disappointed in you." He began fiddling with the coffee filters. "Don't come in on Thursday and Friday. My daughter can cover for you. We'll talk on Monday." He shooed Zoe away with his hand. "I need a few days to think."

She stepped back from him, a death grip on her purse. She wanted to reason with him, to explain, to make him understand she would never destroy his bookstore.

Instead, she walked back to the front door and noticed the results of the break-in. Books covered almost every inch of the floor, creating a crazy patchwork quilt. Displays were turned upside down, and the Halloween decorations were in tatters. She gasped at the pumpkin lights crushed on the floor.

"This is terrible," she muttered. And she was one hundred percent responsible for the destruction since she was the one who failed to set the alarm. Her shoulders sagged, and she blew out a shaky breath.

She noticed Detective Sanders examining the metal frame of the front door. "I'll be off for a couple of days. Do you need my cell number, just in case?"

Understanding brown eyes looked at her. "Just in case of what?"

She halfheartedly brushed hair out of her face. "In

case you have more questions. I want to cooperate with your investigation."

The detective chuckled. "Thanks. Give your number to the patrol officer on the sidewalk." His attention turned back to the door after he said, "And don't leave town."

Chapter Eleven

Zoe drove home and brewed a pot of Yukon Blend coffee. She swallowed four aspirin and considered her choices for breakfast. Food would settle her queasy stomach, keep her hands busy, and her mind empty. She didn't enjoy being ostracized from her job on a Thursday morning. Food would at least be a diversion.

She pulled eggs, bacon, sour cream, tomatoes, and green onions from the refrigerator. While staring at the ingredients huddled together on the granite counter, tears filled her eyes. Her chest began to heave. She rubbed her eyes with her fingers and bent over the counter, praying the toxins would drain out of her brain. "Please, please help me . . . I don't know what to do. I—"

Suddenly, Zoe stood straight. "I will not be a baby. I'm an adult and I'll act like one." She pulled back her shoulders and sucked in her stomach. The pity party was over.

She made an enormous omelet and enjoyed every bite along with wheat-berry toast and raspberry jam. Both her stomach and her head felt better.

After clearing the dishes, she decided to spend the next couple of days doing something useful. She grabbed the notes on Ansel's curse from the study, settled on the sofa, and flipped on the television.

She organized her notes by family, Dodd and Delaney, and reviewed the family trees from Teddy. Several members of the Delaney family currently lived in Houston, including Robert Delaney Sr.

A faint train whistle sounded. Zoe glanced up from the pad of paper on her lap. As he had the previous evening, Ansel sat in the recliner.

"Good morning, Zoe."

"Morning, sorry about last night." She had a somewhat hazy memory of banishing him from the living room. She smiled lamely. "It's good you're here. I'll be spending the next couple of days concentrating on you and your curse."

"I like the sound of you concentrating on me," he said, his eyes flashing. "But seriously, how are you feeling?"

"I'm fine," she said and then for some strange reason decided to tell Ansel the truth. "Actually, I'm not fine at all. I forgot to set the alarm last night at Merlin's. Some jerk broke in the one night I didn't set it."

"That's terrible," he said and rubbed is hands on his thighs and leaned toward her. "Was anyone hurt?"

"No. But the store's a mess. Mr. Allen told me to stay home until Monday." She noticed her hands clenched over the pad of paper. "I guess I better start looking for another job."

"Do the police know who broke in?"

"If they do, they're not telling me." Zoe rose and stood before Ansel. "Let's get back to you and the curse. What do you know about Robert Delaney?"

"Who's that?" Ansel coughed, placing his hand over his mouth.

Duh, of course Ansel wouldn't know. "He was born after you died. Robert is Maxim and Charlotte's child. He's now president of the family business." She grinned, sat on the sofa again, and said innocently. "Wasn't that your old job?"

"Maxim's child is president? Really? I don't believe it." He rose and began pacing. After a few moments he stopped and glared at her. "Do you suppose Maxim was involved in my murder?"

"I don't know, but the thought has crossed my mind."

"What are we going to do about it?'

"You are doing nothing. I'm going to visit your nephew, Robert, and do a little detective work."

Ansel stopped his pacing. "Are you sure that's a good idea? We don't know anything about this Robert person."

"Don't worry, he's a Delaney after all. I'll tell him I'm doing research for my magazine article. Who can resist an opportunity to have a quote in print?"

∼৹

Following a brief Internet search on Robert Delaney, Zoe contacted his office at J&L Manufacturing. She explained her need for an interview to his assistant, who thankfully penciled her name on his schedule. She had two hours before the meeting, enough time for a relaxing bath and another cup of coffee.

She arrived at Robert's office in downtown

Houston right on time and announced herself to the receptionist, who directed her through etched glass double doors to the presidential suite.

Minus the assistant's desk, the waiting room reminded Zoe of the elegant living room at the Dodd house in New Orleans—cherry paneling, causally arranged blue and gold sofas, oriental rugs on oak floors, and a huge wide-screen television in the corner.

Zoe stopped in front of the desk. "I have an appointment with Mr. Delaney at eleven thirty."

"Yes, you do." A white-haired woman with bright red lipstick examined her. "He's on time today. I'll tell him you've arrived. You may enter through that door." She pointed to a wide oak door to her right.

Zoe murmured, "Thank you" before opening the office door. She paused in the doorway to get her bearings. The office was the size of a basketball court, or nearly so. It reflected the same décor as the waiting room, with a bar along one wall. A massive desk filled the far end. A man stepped around it and waited. Robert Delaney was a man accustomed to people coming to him, she concluded quickly and didn't disappoint him.

She reached him with an outstretched hand. "Mr. Delaney, I'm Zoe Miller." They shared a limp handshake. "Thank you for seeing me on such short notice."

"My pleasure." He led her to a pair of striped wing chairs near the window. "May I offer you coffee, tea, something with more bite to it?"

"No, thank you."

"I must tell you my cousin, Sara Ford, told me you

visited her this past weekend. I assume your magazine article relates to my dead uncle."

Zoe nodded. "I'm writing a feature article on ghosts who overstay their welcome."

"How can I help you with that?"

"I'd like to include the Delaney family history in the article."

He raised an eyebrow. "I'm not sure I agree with that."

She raised a hand. "Please, let me explain." He nodded, and she went on. "I've already performed considerable research at the Houston library, including the *Chronicle* archives and a couple of family histories. What I'd like to include is a modern perspective on the events from seventy years ago."

"Like what?"

"For example, Ansel Delany's murder was never solved. Has that fact affected his resilience as a spirit? Has it influenced the family he left behind?"

The office was quiet other than the hum of the air-conditioner. For several moments, Robert looked straight ahead while Zoe fidgeted.

She couldn't handle the silence. "Another point to consider is the potential status of the Whitmire and Delaney families today if Ansel hadn't died prematurely."

"Interesting." He pressed his lips together for a moment and then relaxed and smiled. "I'll answer your questions in order. First, I don't have a clue about Ansel's resilience. Don't care. Second, his death impacted only my grandmother. Everyone else accepted it. And would the family be any different if he hadn't died so young? Of course, there'd be another plate on the table at Thanksgiving."

"I'd like to get a quote or two for the article." Zoe tried another angle. "Did your father ever talk about Ansel?"

"Couldn't avoid it when my grandmother was around." He smirked with disdain. "Ansel was her favorite subject. Bored everyone else, though."

"May I quote you on that?" She swore she saw anger in his eyes.

"Of course not," he said quickly before displaying a social smile. "I was merely thinking out loud."

Thus far the interview was a bust. Zoe's detective skills hadn't secured any real clues to help Ansel. She decided to try another tactic. "One of the old newspaper accounts of his death stated he was the president of J&L Manufacturing when he died. Do you know who replaced him?"

"Yes, my father. He hadn't planned on working for the family business, yet when duty called, he stepped up to the plate."

"Maxim was trained in another field?" Zoe's surprise was genuine.

"He was a full professor of English at Rice University. At the time, he was the youngest professor in their history."

Robert's pride in his father was almost gushy. "Working at the family business wasn't his first love, then," she stated. He looked blankly at her and said nothing. A follow-up question was in order. "Did someone in the family help him to, uh, shift gears from teaching to running a successful business?"

"My father wasn't a dyed-in-the-wool businessman when he became the J&L president. But my step-grandfather, William Whitmire, was a wonderful person and worked hard to groom him as the chief executive."

"Impressive," she said. At last she had hit on a topic Robert would talk about.

"I'd say so. We've grown multiple times over in the last seventy years." His face softened as if he were talking about a child.

"Let me change topics," she said, her last try at playing detective. "Did your grandparents have a good marriage?"

"I suppose so. Isn't that covered in a family history?"

"I'd like to have a personal account of how their relationship might have been affected by your grandmother's curse on Ansel." She leaned toward him a notch. "I thought it might be a good quote for my article."

"Make this your quote." Robert gazed at the ceiling then at Zoe. "Ansel's mother imagined she had a touch of the Irish and pretended to cast spells and curses. The family humored her. We all understood she had no power to set a spell."

"No one believed she had 'special' abilities?"

"Heavens no. In her later years she was a delusional old woman." He frowned and rose. "This is all the time I have, Miss Miller. If you have more questions, call my assistant for another appointment."

She recognized a dismissal and gathered her notes and purse.

At the office door she turned to Robert. "One last question." He stopped midstride and she asked. "Who do you believe killed Ansel?"

"Miss Miller, I know there have been rumors over the years involving my father or step-grandfather. I'm certain no one in my family was responsible for my uncle's death."

"Fair enough." She shook his hand again. "Thank you for your time today. I'll be in touch to confirm the quote I use for the article."

Zoe exited the office with her head high and a dozen questions zigzagging across her brain. She left the building with another idea to help Ansel percolating in her head.

∽

After a quick lunch of a grilled cheese sandwich and potato nuggets at a convenient fast food drive-in on Shepherd, Zoe headed toward the opposite side of Houston. She hadn't consciously known her direction, but after several minutes of driving straight west, she realized her destination was Ansel's grave site. The cemetery was a few miles away. Not a huge distance in a city as geographically spread out as Houston.

After twenty minutes in the zone of sailing through green traffic lights, she reached Forest Lawn Cemetery and turned into the main entrance defined by a massive stone arch. She stopped at the security guardhouse and rolled down the window.

"I need directions to the grave of Ansel Delaney III."

The guard flipped through a black spiral binder. "Delaney, you say?" She nodded. He turned a few pages and ran a finger down one. "What was the first name again?"

"Ansel. A-N-S-E-L."

"Here it is." The guard turned back to her and pointed with a gnarled finger. "Now listen, miss. Go straight down the main road, turn right at the mausoleum building, left at the next road. The Delaney plots are down a bit on the right. Look for a small grove of oak trees." He closed the binder. "Got it?"

She repeated, "Right, left, oak trees." After a couple of wrong turns she spotted the trees, made a quick turn, and rolled to a stop along the edge of the road. She exited the car and leaned against its hood, surveying the grassy area in front of her.

A black wrought iron fence enclosed the oak trees and several large headstones. She walked a few feet to a gate facing the road. The name "Delaney" was fashioned in its scrollwork. After tripping the latch, she entered the burying ground of the Delaney family ancestors.

"I hope no one minds me being here," she muttered. She turned in a full circle, not spying anyone within shouting distance. "Now I'm talking to myself. I need to find Ansel's grave."

A brick walk ran along the inside edge of the fence with each grave perpendicular to it. The backs of the headstones faced the oak trees. After reading the inscription on each marker, Zoe wandered from the foot of one grave to the next. About a quarter of the way around the walk, she came to the site of Ansel's father, Ansel Paul Delaney II: "Beloved son, husband, and father, dedicated to the principles of sportsmanship and fair play – A True Gentleman – 1883 – 1933."

"He died five years before Ansel, at fifty years old," Zoe whispered. "I wonder what caused his death. I'll have to ask Ansel."

The next grave was Ansel's mother, Lucy Lee Delaney-Whitmire—born in 1884 and died in 1988. The headstone was pink marble with an ornate engraving of an angel. "Teddy was right. She did live to be 104 and died exactly fifty years after Ansel—a weird coincidence or intentional?"

She wondered why Lucy chose to be buried next to her first husband rather than the second. Maybe that was the family's decision. Did Maxim insist she be buried with the Delaney's? Or had the Whitmire family balked at including her final resting place in their family plot? Family dynamics could be incredibly complicated.

Zoe moved to the next grave and found Ansel's. Chills crawled up her back. The tombstone was black marble with the inscription "Beloved Son and Brother – Simply the Best – 1905 – 1938." It was magnificent. Zoe pulled a digital camera from her purse and snapped several photos. She noticed a wide green vase filled with white roses sitting next to the headstone. Who sent the flowers? None of the other headstones had a fresh bouquet. *Hmm, another interesting fact for further reflection.*

She continued around the remainder of the brick walk ending at the gate. She hadn't recognized any other names on the markers. Gazing over the Delaney family plot with its center grove of oak trees, her thoughts turned to Ansel and the life he had missed.

True, he was enveloped with his family in death, but what had he missed in life? Surely, being a flesh-and-blood husband, father, and grandfather outweighed the closeness of death with his mother and father. The experience of life was unquestionably meant to exceed the experience of death. Poor Ansel, he didn't have a chance.

She exited the Delaney plot and climbed in her car. She had more questions than answers about Ansel and his family. Why was it that seventy years after Ansel's death, he seemed more alive than dead?

Chapter Twelve

Merlin's opened at noon on Thursday. Everyone, minus Zoe, pitched in to repair the disorder from the burglary in record time. The store was ready for business, and Jill was ready for snooping. She offered an excuse to the front desk clerk and made a beeline for Zoe's office. It was the one area of the store she hadn't fully rummaged through. She searched the desk, two old file cabinets, and every box and corner of the closet. Nothing. No first edition of *The Adventures of Tom Sawyer*.

She pulled her cell phone from the back pocket of her jeans and punched in her brother's number.

"I searched Zoe's office. Nothing. I'm certain the book isn't at Merlin's."

"Thanks, kid. I guess our last hope is the trunk in Zoe's attic," Sam said.

"Not again."

"We don't have another choice. Finding the book is too important. I'll make another date with Zoe to get her out of her house. Stay cool, Jill. This will be over soon."

She clicked off and moved quietly back into the main store. Stay cool. How? Customers were milling around, unaware of the commotion a few hours earlier. She warmly surveyed the repaired Halloween decorations and the shelves of books. After working at the bookstore for two years, Merlin's had become a second home to her.

She didn't agree with her brother's obsession over the gift of a first edition of *The Adventures of Tom Sawyer* to their father on his twenty-fifth birthday. The gift had occurred so many years ago that it was no wonder they couldn't find it in his belongings after his death. Sam was convinced their father gave the book back to Mr. Allen as the result of an argument.

Jill remembered the story Sam had told her. As a teenager, he had overheard a conversation between the two men. He never forgot their argument over the rare version of the book. Both men were collectors of old books and often shared information about editions coming up for auction. Sam mentioned years later the argument seemed so out of character for the two men. They had been good friends since childhood and rarely disagreed on anything other than women.

Jill felt guilty about searching Merlin's on the sly. Both Zoe and Mr. Allen had been so good to her—periodically adjusting her work hours to coordinate with her school schedule and encouraging her to both read and write. Zoe had told her a hundred times that a good author was a great reader. She hoped one day she'd be able to make up the deception to Zoe.

～✺

Zoe drove straight home from the cemetery. She wasn't hungry, so she went straight to the study to surf the Internet. Her curiosity about Robert Delaney and

J&L Manufacturing had been further roused by her visit to downtown Houston. Gaining more information on both seemed like a smart idea. After all, Maxim's child taking the reins of the family business may have been a direct result of Ansel's murder. If Ansel had lived, perhaps his own son would have been the corporate president.

After keying Robert's name into her search engine, several pages of links appeared on the screen. The president of an old and respected Houston business was popular in the local media. Zoe clicked on link after link, carefully reading each document. She learned Robert assumed his current position at J&L on his father's retirement almost thirty-five years ago. He had grown the company from a domestic one to an international supplier of tug boats, tankers, and cargo ships.

Talk about a lousy time for a family member to be involved in a murder. The media would devour the juicy gossip. Maybe Ansel's warning was right, her trip to New Orleans had spooked someone.

"You called."

She turned toward his voice. Ansel lounged in his usual spot on one of the wicker chairs. "How can you hear my thoughts?"

"Simple. That old magic thing." He stretched out his legs. "What are you up to?"

She ignored the old magic comment but decided he had special powers as a ghost, another good topic for an article. "I did a search on your nephew, Robert. He's quite the popular guy around town."

"I know." Ansel frowned and sighed. "I'm not

sure about this modern version of the Delaney family."

"What? How do you know that?"

"Don't get mad at me, but I used your computer yesterday and researched my family."

Zoe shook her head slowly. "Geez, considering all the skills you have, I might force you to get a job to pay rent."

"Very funny. I did it to help you. I must contribute to solving the mystery of my murder."

Zoe snorted. "Good for you. Now back to Robert. He's socially well placed, civic minded, and has grown the Delaney family business into an international powerhouse."

"He sounds a whole lot better than his son, Bobby."

"What are you talking about?"

"Per the society gossip sites, Bobby has a bit of a wandering eye, and his poor wife is very embarrassed about his, uh, escapades."

"Isn't that something? I bet he and/or Robert knew I was in New Orleans. Remember the SUV that tried to run us off the road?"

Ansel nodded. "Maybe father or son Delaney hired that SUV to scare you and your aunt."

"Is it possible you're trying to make a connection when there isn't any proof there is one?"

"I'm not sure. By the way, J&L Manufacturing is in negotiations with the Department of the Army for a half-billion-dollar contract. Wouldn't publicity about a family member's unsolved murder be unwelcome?"

"You have a point." Zoe wagged her index finger at her logically thinking ghost.

"And it would be even more unwelcome if the murderer was a family member."

"Agreed. We can talk about your death, right?" Zoe had her fingers crossed for good luck. She needed this information. "It doesn't relate to the curse."

"Let's give it a try." He rose and began his usual pacing. "Ask any question you want."

What a change from a week ago when he wouldn't talk at all. She wondered what had caused the change but decided not to question it. Some things, one simply accepted.

"You died in the home of Charlotte Dodd. Was she your girlfriend?"

"Good lord, no," Ansel declared. "She had dated Maxim since they were teenagers."

"Then why were you in her house?"

"Because of a stupid mistake."

Zoe's crossed her arms and watched him. "Do fill me in."

"Maxim had broken up with Charlotte a few months earlier. He wasn't ready for marriage, and she was." He looked at the ceiling. "Surely you understand the typical timing issue between men and women?"

"Who hasn't dealt with it?" Bill's face flitted across Zoe's mind.

"We met at a charity ball one weekend by accident, dancing and drinking too much champagne. I took her home and one thing led to another. Two months later, she discovered her pregnancy."

"I'm shocked," Zoe said with a discreet chuckle.

"It wasn't funny." Ansel shook his finger at her. "No one was happy about it, least of all Maxim."

"It seems like so much leads to Maxim."

"I agree. I hadn't thought about that. I can't believe my brother had anything to do with my murder."

"What was your relationship with Maxim?" Zoe had been dying to ask this for days. "Did you get along?"

"He was my little brother, part nuisance, part hero worship." He tapped his chin with a finger. "Close as kids but once I went to college, everything changed."

"Was Maxim jealous of you?"

"I don't know." He shook his head. "I don't think so. Maybe."

"Maybe?"

"Yes, maybe. I was my mother's favorite. She didn't hide it. My father gave Maxim a lot of attention, to make up for it, I think."

"Brothers can be competitive," Zoe suggested. "Was that part of the problem?"

"I think it was because I did everything first, including dying."

"He couldn't have been jealous of that." Zoe couldn't imagine a brother's jealousy resulting in murder. Of course, there was Cain and Able.

"Let's hope not," Ansel agreed.

"But he finally one-upped you. He retired as president of J&L Manufacturing, and you didn't."

"There is that." Ansel stopped his pacing. "Still, I can't believe he wanted me dead simply to take my job. He didn't even like the family business."

"Let's assume the killer wasn't Maxim. Who else would have benefited from you being out of the way?"

Ansel sat again, thumbed his fingers on the arm of the chair, and stared into space. "The only person I can think of was my stepfather."

"What did he have to gain?"

"Control. He was a friend of my father's and always interested in the family business. I remember as a child, William trying to convince my father to take him on as a partner."

"I wonder if his need to be a part of the company got the best of him." Zoe wanted more details on Ansel's murder. "Back to my original question—why did you go to Charlotte's house that day?"

"To talk about the baby, determine a plan of action. Neither of us wanted to get married, but that was what people did back then."

"Society sure had an influence," Zoe muttered. "Who knew you were going to her house?"

"Charlotte, of course, and my secretary, Mildred. She knew my whereabouts at all times."

"Would Mildred have told anyone, say William or Maxim, where you were?"

"The family always had access to my schedule."

"Tell me exactly how your murder happened. Don't leave out a detail."

Ansel returned to the wicker chair, closed his eyes for a few seconds, and then spoke in a soft voice. "I'll tell you what I remember, as best I can."

"Okay, then," she said, waggling a hand at him. "Come on, let's go."

"Bossy woman," Ansel muttered, but then he composed himself by folding his hands over his lap. "I was supposed to meet Charlotte at her house at five thirty in the evening, and I was ten minutes late. I used a key she left under a flowerpot on the front porch."

"She was there?"

"No, the house was pitch-black when I arrived. I hated walking into that silent house, didn't belong there. Anyway, after my eyes adjusted, I moved into what was probably the foyer and finally flipped a light switch."

"Sounds kind of spooky," Zoe suggested.

"It was spooky all right. But the front room was beautiful—silk sofas and Tiffany lamps on fancy tables with an Oriental rug covering a good portion of the dark oak floor. Don't know much about decorating, but I can recognize quality when I see it."

"Thanks for the decorating lesson." She rolled an index finger in front of her chest, motioning for him to continue with his story. "Your murder?"

Ansel nodded. "I heard a noise, something banging upstairs. It was annoying, so I climbed the stairs and turned on the hall light. I walked down the hallway and determined the noise came from a room to the left."

"Would that be the master bedroom?"

"I guess. It's the room you sleep in."

Zoe shivered at the piece of information. But an event over seventy years ago would not freak her out. "Continue with your story."

"I turned on a floor lamp and trotted over to the window and pushed aside the curtains. The noise came from an unlocked window banging against the frame from the wind. I latched the window and heard a floorboard squeak behind me."

"Uh-oh, doesn't sound good."

"It wasn't," Ansel said. "I turned around thinking it was Charlotte. My heart stopped on the spot. It wasn't Charlotte but a man with a rifle in his hands and a bandanna over his face."

"Holy cow, what did you do?"

"I asked the man what he wanted."

"What did he say?" Zoe figured she would have run down the stairs like a bunny rabbit at the sight of the gun.

"Nothing. He pointed the gun at my chest and fired. The bullet pierced directly through my heart. I was dead at its first touch."

"Geez, that's a gruesome story." She itched to reach out and wrap Ansel in a fierce bear hug.

"Yeah, especially the dead part." Ansel rolled his eyes.

"Bummer you didn't recognize the killer." Zoe shivered at the morbid thought and then remembered her visit to the cemetery. "I almost forgot. I took pictures of your grave. I'll get my camera downstairs."

As she stepped on the first floor, the phone rang. She picked it up in the kitchen. "Miss Miller, this is Detective Sanders. I need to speak with you."

"All right, where should I meet you?"

"I'll be at your home in five minutes." The phone clicked off.

Zoe yelled up the stairs. "The police are coming over. Make yourself scarce." She heard chains rattling followed by a door slam. "Good, he heard me."

The doorbell rang in four minutes. Prompt cops. Zoe ushered the detective and a female police officer into her living room.

"Thanks for seeing us on short notice," Detective Sanders said. He pointed to the woman next to him. "This is my partner, Detective Owens."

Zoe nodded to her. "How may I help you?" She motioned the detectives to the sofa, sat in the recliner.

Detective Sanders glanced at his partner. "We need to clarify a couple of items. First, explain the events of yesterday before the break-in at the bookstore."

"Like I told you before, Wednesday was the day I expected to hear about my proposal to buy the store. I was anxious and hoping my offer would be accepted by Mr. Allen. A bit after four, the broker called and gave me the bad news." Zoe's voice trembled as she spoke.

"Were you surprised by the news, or did you have reason to expect it?" Detective Owens asked.

She cleared her throat, "I was totally surprised. The other buyer didn't come into the picture until well after I had submitted my final offer."

"Was there any unusual event around the time you heard about the second offer that comes to mind?" Detective Sander asked this question.

"Let me think. I had lunch with Sam Dodd on Tuesday, heard about the second offer Wednesday night, went to the library with my aunt Thursday afternoon, and had dinner with Sam on Friday night."

"Who's Sam Dodd?"

"He's the brother of Jill, a part-time employee at Merlin's." She tried to lighten the mood. "You know, a cute, single guy."

Both detectives smiled politely. "Your boyfriend?" Detective Owens asked.

"No, our first date was the lunch last week."

"Back to yesterday," Detective Sanders said. "What did you do after you heard the decision?"

"I was stunned by the news, so I probably sat in my office for close to an hour and a half. Once I got my act together, I went out to the main floor of the store. There weren't any customers, so I decided to close ten minutes early. I simply wanted to go home, to escape."

"Why didn't you turn on the alarm?" The detectives were trading questions.

"I was distracted. I forgot." Zoe didn't know how else to explain the truth.

"Anything else you'd like to tell us?" the female detective asked.

Zoe thought for a moment. "One unusual event is that my house was broken into this past weekend. It happened while I was out of town."

Detective Owens perked up. "Did you call the police?"

"Yes, and the officer filed a report. It was weird, though. My belongings were torn apart, but nothing was taken."

"I'll follow up on that," Detective Sanders said while frowning. "By the way, have you talked to Mr. Allen today?"

"No. Was I supposed to call him?" Zoe hadn't planned on talking with Mr. Allen until Monday.

"We don't know. He may file charges against you for—"

"What?" Her chest tightened. This couldn't be true. "What are you talking about? He has no reason to file charges."

～～

Robert Delaney Sr. poured two fingers of McAllen eighteen-year-old scotch into a Waterford tumbler. The single ice cube chilled the liquid, providing the perfect sipping temperature. He downed one finger in a single swallow.

"Hey, Dad. Thirsty?"

Robert turned from the bar and gazed at oldest son, Robert Jr., fondly called Bobby by close friends and family. At forty years old, he was at the top of his game—handsome, a successful businessman, and a devoted father and husband. Though, his one flaw, the lack of integrity, tended to overshadow his many good points. Yet no one would have the nerve to criticize his dedication to J&L Manufacturing.

"May I offer you a drink?" Robert poured, offered his son a tumbler of scotch without expecting an answer to his question. He gestured to the wing chairs by the window. "We need to talk."

"What's the mystery?" Bobby followed his father's suggestion and settled into a chair. "You sounded secretive on the phone."

"Sorry about that." Robert looked out the window before facing his son. "How close are we to the final agreement?"

"The latest draft is on the desk of the head of budgets at the Department of the Army. I hope this will be the last one. We ought to be a few days away from signing the contract."

"Good. Let me know when you hear back from them." Robert rose and began to plod a path between the window and the bar. He stopped to address his son. "We may have a potential problem that could create negative publicity."

Bobby raised an eyebrow. "A problem? About what?"

Robert glared at his son. "What did we discuss over the weekend?"

"You can't be serious." Bobby sucked in a healthy slug of scotch. "Who cares about some bookstore clerk asking questions about some relative who croaked over seventy years ago?"

"She's becoming a nuisance, asking too many damn questions. I may be forced to do something stronger than road rage on a freeway."

"I already took care of that," Bobby said confidently. "Arranged a little break-in at that bookstore she works at. Figure she'll get fired and have something else to think about besides a Delaney murder that occurred eons ago."

"That's a terrible thing to do." Robert was torn between being proud of Bobby's resourcefulness and appalled at his lack of integrity. "It might make her even more curious about the murder."

"Cool it, Dad. So what if Ansel's murder was never solved. It's old news. Who cares now besides that little twit?"

"I do. I know who killed your great-uncle."

Chapter Thirteen

Zoe directed the detectives out her front door and went to the kitchen for a glass of green tea when the phone rang. "Not the police again," she muttered.

"Zoe, it's Mom. You need to come to the emergency room at Memorial City Hospital."

"What's going on?"

"Your father had a spell, and I brought him here to get checked out."

"Is he okay?" Zoe asked, her heart pounding.

"Just get here."

Her mouth dry and her stomach rolling, Zoe raced to her bedroom to change into jeans and a sweater. Within two minutes of her mother's call, she opened her car with a click of the door lock. After carefully backing out of the driveway, she punched the accelerator. The tires squealed as she braked at the corner.

"Ouch, I better slow down. I don't need a ticket or an accident." Zoe swung into traffic, heading for the nearest freeway.

Thirty minutes later, minus any vehicular calamity, she ran into the hospital's emergency room. She stopped ten feet inside the glass doors, frantically searching for her mother's face among those scattered around the waiting area. Nothing. She hurried to the information desk.

"My father is here, David Miller," Zoe announced. "Please, please tell me where he is."

"You're Zoe?" A white-haired woman with tired eyes asked.

"Yes, ma'am."

"Your father's in room 2-B." She gestured to her left. "Register at the desk and then go through those doors. The room is at the end of the hall."

Zoe scribbled her name in a notebook, barreled through the doors, and raced down the hallway. She found the room and silently watched her parents from the doorway. Toni's back faced the door as she bent over her sleeping husband. She held his hand and stroked his hair. Love welled in Zoe's heart. She rubbed her face and adjusted her ponytail.

Zoe coughed, said in a small voice, "Mom, I'm here."

Toni shoulders relaxed and she turned toward her daughter. Worry etched her eyes. "Hi, baby, sorry to ruin your evening."

"What's wrong with Dad?"

"Let's go out in the hallway." Toni took Zoe by the arm.

Once they stood in an alcove a few feet away from the room, Toni hugged her daughter. "I'm glad you're here."

"You're scaring me. What's going on?"

Toni took a deep breath, blinked back tears. She shook her head, visibly straightened her torso. "Your father has a heart problem."

"What type of problem?" A picture of her sweat-soaked father after a five-mile run flashed through Zoe's mind.

"The doctors aren't sure how serious it is. An angioplasty is scheduled at ten tomorrow morning."

"Is that serious?" Zoe braced herself for her mother's answer.

"The procedure is common." Toni squeezed her arm. "They'll look for a blockage. If it's not too bad, they'll put in a stent. If it's bad, then he'll need surgery."

"What can I do to help?"

"Stay with me. We're waiting to be transferred to a room." Toni glanced toward the ER room. "Let's check on your father."

A nurse met them at the entrance.

"We have a room for Mr. Miller. In a moment we'll transfer him to 19A on the eighth floor. Y'all can go ahead, and we'll meet you there."

"Are you sure?" Toni asked.

"We have a secret shortcut." She winked, waved to an orderly at the opposite end of the hall.

Toni gave her husband a kiss on the cheek before taking her daughter's arm and guiding her out of the ER room and through a door into the east wing of the hospital.

"Do you want a soda or a cup of coffee?" Toni asked. They were in front of the hospital's cafeteria.

Zoe shook her head.

"I need coffee. Wait here."

Zoe watched her mother thread her way through

the people milling around the various food bars. She lost sight of her behind the dessert counter. Zoe stationed herself against a wall, which provided an excellent view of visitors and hospital employees. Each person who crossed in front of her was no doubt on a personal journey. With any luck, it was one of their own choosing. A hospital was a terrible place to philosophize about a person's life since so often that life might be in jeopardy. What a morbid thought. She watched a young couple push a baby stroller. Her heart tugged. That was the real deal. Someday, hopefully someday, that would be her.

Toni returned with two tall cups.

"They have Starbucks, so I figured you'd want a latte."

Zoe accepted the cup. "Thanks."

"Come on." Toni pulled her daughter to the left. "We need to follow this hallway to the main lobby. The elevator to the patient rooms is over there."

"How do you know your way around here, Mom?"

"This is where Nana died, sweetheart."

"I remember now." Zoe could have kicked herself. Forgetting where her grandmother was so ill and had died was unforgivable. Her brain had lost its power to think beyond the moment.

They walked through the long corridor to the main hallway of the hospital, their shoes squeaking on the shiny tile floor. They turned right and shortly came to the elevators. Toni pushed the correct button.

They exited on the eighth floor and followed the signs to room 19A. Sure enough, David had already arrived and was awake. They entered and planted themselves on either side of his bed.

He turned to Zoe. "Thanks for coming, baby. Sorry your old man is such a hassle.

Zoe kissed his cheek. "You're never a hassle, a pain maybe." She grinned and patted his arm. "How are you feeling?"

"Silly mostly. I eat fiber regularly and run three miles a day. Why do I have heart problems?"

"Now David, you know some things just happen." Toni straightened the hair over his forehead. "Let's wait until tomorrow and we have the results of your test. It may not be serious at all."

"I agree with Mom. We need all the facts."

"That reminds me, have you heard about your offer for Merlin's?" Toni asked, searching her daughter's face.

"Mr. Allen accepted the second offer."

"What the hell? Did he give you a reason?" David asked.

"No reason. I guess he liked the other proposal better." Zoe looked from one parent to the other. "That's not the worst of it. When I left the store last night, I forgot to set the alarm. Naturally, someone broken in. Just my luck it happened on the one night I didn't set the alarm."

David struggled to sit up while Toni fluffed the pillow. "Was anyone hurt?"

"No, and it appears nothing was taken. The police detective told me Mr. Allen may file charges against me."

Toni moved around the end of the bed to hug her

daughter. "Oh, sweetie, I am so sorry."

"I don't know, Zoe." David sounded doubtful. "He was probably just angry. Mr. Allen isn't the sort of man to file charges simply because someone makes a mistake."

"I hope you're right," Zoe said.

Zoe stayed with her parents for another hour and then kissed each one goodnight and headed back home. She'd return the next morning in time for her father's procedure.

Walking in her front door, she found Ansel pacing in the living room.

He stopped when he saw her. "What's going on?"

"My father's in the hospital." Zoe dropped her purse on the sofa. "I need a snack." In the kitchen she grabbed guacamole and a can of lemon tea from the refrigerator and a bag of tortilla chips from the pantry.

She plopped on the recliner. Ansel watched her for a second and couldn't help but make a comment on her snack. "That doesn't look like healthy food."

"I need comfort food right now, not vegetables."

"How's your father?" Ansel said.

"He's having a procedure tomorrow to check out his heart. Either he'll need stents or surgery."

"Stents?"

"I'm too tired to explain." Zoe munched on a chip and enjoyed the coldness of the tea. "Remember earlier when I mentioned my visit to your grave today."

He nodded.

She found her purse on the sofa and dug out the camera. "I took pictures for you." She showed him how to push the small button on the camera to display each image. "I included the graves of your parents and Maxim, too. It's a nice setting."

"This is surreal," Ansel noted as he moved through the images. "I can't believe I'm looking at my own grave."

"I can't believe I'm talking to a ghost who's checking out pictures of his grave on my twenty-first century camera."

"This is a weird situation for both of us." He looked closely at the camera. "Those are fresh roses by my headstone. Who would be sending flowers now?"

Zoe remembered the white roses in the beautiful urn. "I wondered about that, too."

"Perhaps it's a clue," Ansel suggested. "Can we find out where they came from?"

"I will try." She stabbed a finger at him. "You, stay off the phone and do not try to use the Internet."

Ansel saluted. "Yes, ma'am." He continued with the camera. "The message on my father's tombstone is so accurate: A True Gentleman. He was the kindest and most intelligent person you'd ever have the pleasure to know. We missed him after his death."

"I hope I'm not prying, but how did he die?"

"Zoe, it was almost eighty years ago. Remember you can ask me any question you wish—"

"Except the curse."

"Except the curse," Ansel confirmed. "Dad died after a riding accident. He was exercising his favorite thoroughbred, Jasper, at the family stables. For some reason he fell off and his head hit a rock."

"Was he an experienced rider?" Zoe figured being inexperienced was a logical reason for a riding accident.

"Yes. He was a member of the Olympic equestrian team in 1924. We figured the horse got spooked and threw him off. He wasn't found until Jasper came back without him."

"That must have been horrible for your mother," Zoe said.

"It was a dreadful time. William Whitmire helped Mother with all the details."

"He sounds like a real stand-up guy," Zoe said while rolling her eyes. "How long before they were married?"

"Three years."

"And then two years later you're dead."

"That may not be a coincidence," Ansel said, tapping a finger against his lower lip. "Whitmire was a powerful man. He could have easily hired my killer."

"Another possibility. I need to think about this." Zoe yawned.

After checking her watch, she gathered the remnants of her snack and deposited them in the kitchen. "I'm going to bed. Please don't wake me in the morning." She started up the stairs. "Don't try to take any pictures with the camera. Your magic would probably screw it up."

"Bossy woman," he muttered.

"I heard that."

Zoe changed into her jammies and snuggled into bed thinking about Ansel and his family. As was becoming the norm for her, her unconscious thoughts turned into another dream with Ansel as the star.

"Hurry up, Zoe," Ansel hollered to the closed

bathroom door. "The blackjack tables are calling out to me."

A knock at the door of their hotel suite distracted him.

"Room service, sir." A waiter pushed a cart holding a champagne bucket, glasses, and a bowl of strawberries along with a small dish of whipped cream.

"You've got the wrong room," Ansel told the waiter.

"No, he doesn't." Zoe stood behind him and nodded to the waiter. "Thanks for being so quick. Ansel, give the man a tip."

He followed her instructions, closed the door, and slowly turned.

While in the bathroom, Zoe had called room service, changed into a black negligee, and managed to erase four hours of traveling time from Houston to Las Vegas. By the gleam in his eye, she knew her efforts were appreciated.

"Babe, you look good enough to eat."

Zoe walked toward him with a seductive swing to her hips. "I thought we might relax for a bit before we hit the tables." She reached for his belt. "Gambling can be stressful." She kissed the corner of his mouth. "Let's snuggle on the bed so you—" She kissed his ear. "—can relax."

"Sounds good to me." He pulled her by the hand, and they fell on the king-size bed.

Two hours later, they sat side by side at a blackjack table in the main casino section of Caesar's Palace. Zoe thought the minimum bet of twenty-five dollars was a bit rich for her budget, but Ansel was loaded now, so what the hell. An hour later they walked away from the table, up five thousand dollars between them.

"You're my good luck charm." Ansel threw his arm over her shoulder and gave her a quick squeeze. "Let's get a glass of wine."

"Excellent idea."

They sat along the long oak bar at the Silver Dollar Saloon. Ansel ordered the most expensive merlot available. "Don't know why I like this wine so much." He twirled the glass in front of his face. "It's almost like I can't help myself."

Zoe winked. "Who knows? Perhaps you learned to like it in a former life."

"Maybe so. The same former life where I fell in love with you."

"And I with you."

~∾

Zoe woke the next morning feeling rested and ready for action. While enjoying a second cup of coffee in the kitchen, the phone rang.

"It's Mom. I've got news for you."

"How's Dad? I was just about to leave."

"No need to. We're leaving soon. They did the test an hour ago—"

"What?"

"There was a cancellation. Anyway, it showed a slight blockage in one spot that can be handled with medication."

"That's fantastic. I suppose he'll have to watch his diet."

"You bet. I'm taking your father to a nutritionist whether he likes it or not. We're waiting for the release from the doctor, and then we'll head for home."

"Let me know if you need anything. I'll stop by later today."

Hot damn, Zoe thought, finally some good news. Now her life could get back on track. She poured more coffee and carried the mug to her study.

At the computer, she opened the magazine article's document file. She read the last paragraph she had written.

Not bad. The article had a certain flair. Solving Ansel's curse was a great how-to example for ridding a house of a spirit. She began to type.

My ghost, I'll call him Alfred, was murdered in the 1930s. He died in my house, in the master bedroom to be exact. His intermediary state is my attic. He's not all that annoying and can be entertaining at times, yet he deserves everlasting peace just like the rest of us. Another benefit of his eternal peace is my transformation of the attic into my study. Thus, he's got to go.

Alfred's murder was never solved, which is a problem in itself. But the real issue is that a curse was placed on him by his mother. It's the force of the curse that keeps him roosting in my attic. I've asked him the details more than once. Unfortunately, part of the curse is that he can't talk about it. If I want my attic ghost-free, I have to figure out the curse on my own, minus any assistance from Alfred.

Thank heavens for being able to do research at the

local public library and on the Internet.

The library, of course—gaining access to Lucy's diaries might be the key to understanding the curse. The more she thought about it, the more convinced Zoe became that reading all the diaries would provide the perfect answer for breaking the curse. A passage might provide the identity of Ansel's murderer. She'd need Teddy's help to get into the archives area, as it was restricted from the public.

She phoned Aunt Tina, who thankfully, answered. They agreed to meet at the Black Lab on Montrose in a couple of hours. Zoe continued to work on the article until she left for the restaurant.

Zoe found her aunt at the restaurant's pub style bar enjoying a Bloody Mary. Zoe kissed her on the cheek. "Has the weekend started already?"

"I'm celebrating." Aunt Tina patted the stool next to her. "I just sold a sculpture to a bank downtown, and for a hefty price."

"That's wonderful." Zoe caught the bartender's eye. "I'll have an iced tea." She turned to her aunt. "I heard from Mr. Allen, it's a no go."

Aunt Tina's mouth dropped. "I can't believe that. You've kept that place afloat for the last three years." She surveyed her niece's face. "Anything else going on?"

"Well, yes. When I left on Wednesday night I forgot to turn on the alarm, and the store was burglarized. Mr. Allen may file charges against me."

"That mean old man."

"Aunt Tina, he's not mean." Zoe's eyes welled

with tears, and she blinked them back. "He's mad at me, that's all."

Tina rubbed Zoe's back. "Sweetie, I know. I'm sure this will work out the way it should."

Zoe brushed her eyes and grinned. "That's what you always say."

"When have I ever been wrong?"

Zoe squeezed her aunt's hand. "If I haven't told you lately, I love you, Auntie."

"Same here, sweet pea."

The bartender served Zoe's tea and set menus on the scarred bar. "Let me know when you're ready to order."

"I'm starved," Zoe announced. "I'll have a blue cheeseburger and fries, and vanilla ice-cream for dessert."

"Ditto for me."

While inhaling her lunch and savoring the superb flavor of vanilla ice cream with fudge sauce, an idea gelled in Zoe's mind. She crossed her fingers, hoping her aunt would agree with her plan.

"Auntie, I need your help with something. I'd prefer Teddy's help, but I don't want to involve him. I figure you're the next-best thing."

Tina lowered her head, and her eyes zeroed in on her niece. "I know that tone. You're up to something. What do you need help with?"

Zoe smiled sweetly. "Not much. Let's break into the archives of the Houston Public Library, after hours, of course."

"Is that all?"

Chapter Fourteen

Zoe stopped by her parents' house after lunch. Both were at home, watching television in the family room.

"You don't look half bad," Zoe remarked to her father.

"Thanks, I think." David smiled, though his eyes looked tired. "Tina called a few minutes ago to tell us your news. Again, we're sorry about Merlin's."

Toni rose from the sofa and hugged her daughter who stood in the middle of the room. "Don't worry about all this. Everything will turn out just as it should."

"So I've been told." Zoe rolled her eyes and turned to her father. "Tell me how you're feeling, the real deal this time."

After assurance from both parents that her father was on the mend and would diligently take his medication as prescribed, Zoe headed for home. In two hours, Sam would arrive for another home-cooked meal. She needed to get busy.

The phone rang as she entered her house. She managed to pick it up in the kitchen and smiled at Sam's voice.

"I have bad news. I can't make our date tonight."

"I'm so sorry," Zoe said and meant it. "Is something wrong?"

"No, I'm coming down with a cold. I hope we can reschedule."

"Of course. Take care of yourself."

She slowly replaced the receiver. Damn. She'd been looking forward to the date and a relaxing evening with a handsome man. Poor Sam. Well, she'd do what she always did when she needed to relax—cook.

After changing into comfortable clothes, she selected a bottle of cabernet from the under-counter cellar, uncorked it, and poured a glass. While sipping the wine, she decided to go ahead and make the dinner she had planned for Sam.

She snapped her fingers. "Pasta primavera and Caesar salad coming up."

After gathering the ingredients, Zoe turned on the small television in the corner of the long kitchen counter. It seemed like the perfect opportunity to hear the local evening news, something she rarely had time for.

She gathered the necessary pot and bowl with a cutting board and chef's knife. The vegetables were quickly handled, so she started the burner under the water for the penne pasta. Half listening to the news, she heard the words "J&L Manufacturing" and turned to watch the local anchor.

"Welcome back. J&L Manufacturing announced today they are one of the two finalists for a multimillion dollar contract with the Department of the

Army. If the company signs the ten-year agreement, they estimate five thousand jobs will be added to the Houston economy. It's the largest privately owned company in Texas. In other business news . . ."

Zoe tuned out the anchor. She'd had no idea Ansel's family business was so large. Each family member must be worth millions. Something she'd want to protect if she were a Delaney, but at what personal cost?

"Were you thinking about me?" Ansel sat on the stool several feet from the stove.

She assumed he would appear that evening. At least she hoped so. Even though she had some great ideas for redecorating the attic, she knew she'd miss his presence in her house. Strange how easily he had become a constant in her life in such a short time. Yep, it was his charm.

"You're such comedian. I was thinking about the Delaney family. It looks like J&L is closer to getting that government contract."

"Good for them." Ansel's pride in his family's accomplishments was obvious.

"I wonder if it's all on the up-and-up," Zoe murmured.

"What does that mean?"

She looked at him sharply but saw nothing unusual in his eyes. "It means, I wonder if they've made it this far in the negotiations through one hundred percent legal and ethical means."

"Why would you think otherwise?" He rose and crossed the kitchen to her. "Is there something you haven't told me?"

"No, but I got a strange vibe around Robert. He was polite and answered my questions, yet he seemed, mmm, brittle."

"Brittle. Now that's an interesting word to describe a Delaney." Ansel laughed and slapped his thigh. "Maybe he thought you were being nosy."

"Nosy." Sparks flew from Zoe's eyes. "Here I am trying to help you, and you—"

"I'm sorry. Please, let's not argue," he said softly.

"You're right. I'm so touchy these days." She turned back to washing the lettuce. "I've allowed myself two days to wallow in a pity party about Merlin's. Plan B starts tomorrow."

"Go girl. That's the spirit." He moved a hand toward her shoulder as if to pat it, but stopped himself. "How easily you transcend such a disappointment is a true sign of your character."

"Yep, that's me, full of character," Zoe said with a half-assed grin. "And my plan for breaking and entering tomorrow afternoon is icing on the cake."

Ansel's mouth dropped. "What are your talking about, little missy?"

Zoe burst out laughing. "Little missy? What are you, a 103?"

He stared at her for a moment. "No, in human terms I'm around a hundred and one, or maybe, two." He grinned. "Look good for my age, don't I?"

"Seriously, Ansel, must I remind you that you're dead?"

"You remind me constantly."

"I'm sorry, but remember when we looked at pictures of your grave? That's dead to me."

"All right, all right, let's talk about something else." He pointed to a bowl on the counter. "You're baking a cake? I always liked spice cake with white frosting."

She began to tear lettuce into the salad bowl and then turned her attention to the pasta pot. "I'm not baking a cake. But do keep your smart comments to yourself when I tell you what I am doing." She filled the pot with cold water and placed it on the stove. "Aunt Tina and I are breaking into the private archives section of the Houston library downtown."

"Why and what for? Doesn't Tina have a friend who works there?"

"Yes, but we don't want him involved." She threw him an "Are you an idiot?" look. "We're doing this on our own, with the small addition of Teddy's security code."

"He's helping you after all."

"No, he won't even be there."

Ansel raised his hands in surrender. "Fine. I know you well enough that I can't talk you out of this insane plan, so please be careful."

Zoe examined the contents of her refrigerator. She sensed Ansel's eyes on her back. His gaze was intense, especially for a dead guy. She turned back to him. "All right, what is it? I can feel that you're itching to tell me something."

A glimpse of pain crossed his face but vanished in a nanosecond. Zoe cocked her head, noticing his every blink, and wondered about the outcome of lifting Ansel's curse. She hoped it would provide him the peace he deserved. Not for the first time, she wished he were alive and available. No doubt about it, he was a hunk, especially for a dead guy.

"I just want you to be careful. It's not the end of the world if I'm stuck in your attic for another decade or two." Ansel sat at the bistro table, stretching his muscular legs in front of him.

"Message received. We'll be good little careful burglars." Zoe threw the pasta into the boiling water. "You were thirty-three when you died. Why weren't you married or at least had a steady girlfriend?"

"My heavens, isn't that a little personal?"

"You regularly visit my bedroom. Your point?"

"Point understood," Ansel replied with a sheepish grin. "My life was complicated."

"That's a reason?" She stirred the penne. "Everyone I know has a complicated life. I figure that's the way it's meant to be." She shrugged her shoulders. "Otherwise, it would be plain boring."

"Boring is bad?"

"Ansel, stop. I don't want to discuss the philosophy of life with you." Zoe paused for a moment and then continued. "Tell me about your life seventy years ago."

"My life," Ansel said and looked down at his clasped hands and flexed his fingers, "was good. My family was great, my job was great, and my friends were great." His grin was no longer sheepish, but sexy and arrogant. "I had it all."

Zoe looked at him sharply. "Earth to Ansel, you're sounding cocky."

"I suppose I was back then. Being murdered at thirty-three has a way of changing a person." He obviously realized the simplicity of his words as he chuckled. "What I mean is that I was on a high back then. At least, I thought I was. Now, I'm not so sure. My stepfather was a bad influence on me. In fact, I saw an Internet article about him and gambling debts."

"Interesting," Zoe commented. "If you had the chance, what would you have done differently?"

"Let me think for a minute."

While Ansel stared into space, Zoe assembled her dinner. She drained the pasta and dumped it in a large bowl. After adding the chopped vegetables, she drizzled olive oil over the mixture, followed by fresh lemon juice and minced basil. She gave it a taste before adding a sprinkle of salt and grated fresh pepper. She gave the primavera one last toss and carried it and the salad to the table. She sat across from Ansel.

"No wine?" Ansel said.

"Thanks for reminding me. I poured a glass of cabernet earlier."

"Cabernet is a good wine. I remember it."

Zoe rose and retrieved her glass from the counter. "It is a shame you can't enjoy this," she said as she held up the glass. She noticed the regret in his eyes, and her heart opened. Every cube of ice had melted. *I could love this ghost if he were a man.*

That thought surprised the hell out of Zoe even though she knew it to be true. But it did resolve one thing—neutralizing the curse was now her top priority.

Once again seated across from Ansel, she took a bite of the pasta. "This is good." She glanced at him, "Sorry. I'm happy my recipe turned out so well."

"You develop your own recipes?"

She nodded. "I love it. It's right up there with books on my top-ten list."

They were silent while she munched and he watched her munch.

Ansel spoke first. "I am sorry your proposal to buy the bookstore didn't work out. I was thinking though, not buying Merlin's might turn out to be for the best. I'm sure there are many other opportunities available."

"No way. Losing Merlin's is the worst thing that's happened in my life."

Ansel raised his hands. "Please, let me explain."

"Explain."

"My motto is, was, that when something bad happens, another door usually opens. For you, it's the opportunity to create a bookstore of your own choosing."

"You mean open a brand-new bookstore?" Her eyes widened and her mouth opened.

"That's exactly what I mean. Why not combine your top two loves, books and cooking?"

She snapped her mouth shut and looked at him, all the while pondering his idea, a damned good idea. But she didn't know squat about starting a new business.

"I've never thought about opening a new store. Where would I get the money? I don't know. I'll have to think about this and talk to my dad." She worked on the pasta. "In the meantime, let's get back to you and our earlier conversation. If you had the opportunity, what in your life would you do differently?"

"That's a question the average person never has an opportunity to answer." He paused, his eyes staring at the travertine tile on the kitchen floor. "I suppose there are a couple of things I'd do differently."

"Just a couple?"

"I'd rather concentrate on the major ones." He rose and began to pace the small kitchen.

Zoe watched his back-and-forth movement. "Come on, you're avoiding the question. Let's talk."

He stopped and returned to the table. "You're right. It's not an easy thing for a man to admit he made a major mistake last week, let alone seven decades ago."

"Most mistakes can be corrected. Once the curse is lifted and you're settled, I'll fix the mistakes for you as best I can. That's the least I can do, considering what a lousy deal you got." She wanted to squeeze his hand but didn't even try. "Being murdered really sucks."

He beamed. "You're a stand-up person, Zoe Miller."

"Yeah, that's me, number one Girl Scout. Tell me what mistakes I'll be correcting."

"My biggest mistake was listening to my stepfather about the day-to-day management of J&L." His fists clenched. "My father started the company as a young man. He had a knack for business and for knowing the market. Within five years of its opening day, the company was successful and growing. The employees came first, and the bottom line was second."

"You must have loved your father a great deal."

"I respected him as well, the opposite of my stepfather. After his death, I was unsure of my ability to step into his role at J&L, but I did it. I was young and hadn't been involved in running the business long enough to know what to do. Long story short, I listened to William and put the bottom line first. I made a huge mistake, even though the company grew."

"You're not the first young person to listen to the wrong advice." She put her head in her hands and concentrated for a moment. She raised her head. "I'm not sure what I can do now to fix this. I guess I'll need to do more research on the company and learn about the corporate culture and how J&L's employees are treated. I can always write an article if the company isn't what your father would have liked."

"That's a good plan." He gazed at her intently. "I do hope you realize how much I appreciate everything you're doing for me and for my family, even though they don't realize it."

Zoe's heart opened a notch wider. "It's my pleasure. You're a good guy, Ansel Delaney. Too bad your type of man isn't around today. Every single girl in Houston would be after you."

"That I don't think so." His face seemed paler than usual. "To continue, my second major mistake concerns Maxim."

"That doesn't surprise me."

"I thought you'd say that. The truth is, I wasn't a good big brother. I knew my mother favored me over Maxim, and I used that to get my way. I acted like a spoiled brat much of the time."

"All children do that with a sibling at one time or another."

"Perhaps so, but I could have been such a better

brother to him. Looked out for him and taught him how to play baseball and tennis. And going to bed with Charlotte was simply unforgivable." He shook his head and muttered, "A terrible, terrible mistake."

"Not entirely. You did have a son. His name was John," she gently reminded Ansel.

"Right, a son who never met his real father."

"That's true. There is something else to consider. More than likely, your son had a family of his own. Wouldn't it be something if, right now, you have descendants living in Houston?"

～～

Early Saturday morning, Zoe brewed a pot of Komodo Dragon Blend and carried a coffee urn to the study. She poured a mug and pulled out the family trees from Teddy.

She set aside the Delaney tree and focused on the one for the Dodd family. Charlotte's child, John D. Dodd, was born in 1939, before she married Maxim. Ansel's name wasn't listed as the father. She wondered if he'd considered Maxim his father even though they didn't share the same last name. He married Jane Louise Parker in 1972, followed by the births of two children, Sam in 1974 and Jill in 1982.

What?

Zoe gasped. Her skin tingled. Sam and Jill Dodd? The same Sam Dodd who had canceled their dinner date last night? She'd never even thought about his last name being the same as Ansel's Charlotte. If Sam was John Dodd's son, that meant, holy shit, Ansel was Sam's grandfather.

Her mind twirled. Could this be true? She quickly

reminded herself she had no proof Sam was Charlotte and Ansel's grandson. How could she find out the truth? She didn't know the year Sam was born, or Jill for that matter. Should she call either of them and ask? How would she explain her reason for asking? Jill's information might be on her employment application, but that was in the file cabinet in her office at Merlin's, from whence she was banned until Monday. Maybe there was an online source. Or perhaps the Dodd family history at the library would have the information.

Zoe began to wonder if she had missed her calling as a librarian or a detective. She dug a pad of paper from a drawer to make a list of facts to check out at the library. Number one was Lucy's diary and details of Ansel's curse. She wished she had one of those cute miniature spy-type cameras to capture the pages. She jotted a couple more notes, folded the paper to later stow in her purse. She had fifty-eight minutes to get ready and pick up Aunt Tina. Whistling, she headed for her shower.

~⁊

"Zoe, stop. Do you hear footsteps?" Aunt Tina placed her hand on Zoe's arm, halting their progress toward the main door of the genealogy section at the Houston Public Library. They both strained their ears for the echo of footsteps on the marble floor.

She glanced at Aunt Tina. "Move. Someone's coming." She pointed to a couple of light gray cubicles on the left side of the wide hallway. They ducked behind the outside wall just as a security guard came into view at the opposite end of the corridor.

Tina managed to squeeze between two metal bookcases while Zoe ducked under a cubicle desk. The consistent plodding of the guard's leather-soled shoes against the floor should have set off the fire alarm. After what seemed like an hour, she peeked around the edge of the desk and saw the guard exit the hallway through a stairway door.

Zoe crawled out from under the desk and spied her aunt. "He's gone. Let's get this show on the road."

They met in the corridor outside the door to the genealogy room.

"Okay, let's get this over with." Tina moved her eyes from left to right. "You have the key code, right?"

"Yes, ma'am." On the security keypad, Zoe punched in the five numbers provided by Teddy. A soft buzz sounded, and she pushed the door handle down until it gave way. "Come on, we've gotta be quick."

Once inside the genealogy library, Zoe was momentarily at a loss. She'd never expected to enter the hallowed row on row of private bookshelves without limits. It was exhilarating. She felt in total control of her surroundings without a map.

"Auntie, we need to find the family histories and diaries. You were here with Teddy. Do you remember their location?"

Tina looked around the space. Zoe prayed she'd gain her bearings.

"I remember catching a great view of Teddy's butt." Tina's eyes closed for a moment in concentration. She slowly walked a few steps down the space between the stacks. "He turned right, about here." She pointed and disappeared.

Zoe had been reading a notice describing the proper method to trace a family history she'd found taped to the end of a stack. "What?" She turned toward her aunt's voice. "Aunt Tina, where are you?"

Tina's head poked around the corner of a bookshelf. "Over here. I found the books."

Zoe rushed to follow her aunt through the stacks. She turned left and then right, keeping her aunt's back in sight. Suddenly, Aunt Tina stopped and pointed to a shelf above her head. "All the family histories are here with Charlotte and Lucy's diaries." She looked back at her niece. "How do you want to do this?"

Zoe silently counted the histories and diaries: twenty-three, too many to go through in a couple of hours. The key to their search was a directed focus.

"We need to pay attention to the right years. Histories only after 1937, since Ansel died in 1938. Look for a reference in the Whitmire history about J&L Manufacturing and gaining control of it, and anything about Ansel's death." She pulled one of Lucy's diaries off the shelf. "I'll go through the diaries."

They each grabbed an armful of books and settled at a library table near a window. Zoe pulled notebooks and pens out of her purse. "Here, use this to take notes. Be sure to write down which volume you're taking notes from. You never know, we may need to prove where we got our information."

"Even though we did it illegally?" Tina asked.

"Yes, ma'am," Zoe said and got down to business. "We're thorough library burglars. Remember, we're looking for entries related to: Ansel's death, William Whitmire, Charlotte and Maxim's wedding, and the birth of their son John."

"Aye, aye, captain." Aunt Tina giggled and saluted.

Zoe and Tina concentrated on the books for three hours, causing cramped fingers and stiff necks. Each of them had filled several pages in their notebooks.

"I think we've pushed our luck as far as we can," Zoe said, rubbing the back of her neck.

"I agree," replied Tina. "Let's escape."

They reshelved the books and retraced their steps to the entrance. Zoe stepped out of the double doors and peered in both directions. No guard in sight.

"I'll set the alarm, and then we need to get to the elevator fast." Aunt Tina nodded, and Zoe punched in the code to set the alarm. She stashed the paper in the pocket of her jeans and opened the door. "Come on, let's get out of here."

Tina made sure the door was firmly shut. They sprinted effortlessly down the hall to the elevator. Zoe punched the down button while looking in both directions. They were safe. The doors opened, and they entered the elevator. Tina hit the button for the first floor.

"Hey, there. Stop."

"That must be the security guard," Zoe said. The doors closed, and the elevator began its descent. "When we get to the first floor, we need to move quickly away from the elevator. I think there's a section for new releases to the right side, so let's go there. Act like you're searching for a book. He didn't see us, so try to act normal."

"No problem, sweetie. I love spy stuff."

"We're not spies," Zoe said, rolling her eyes.

"Close enough for me." Aunt Tina grinned as the doors opened.

The library's main floor was crowded with families and students. Zoe nodded to her aunt and wandered over to the shelves of new releases. She saw a security guard round the corner toward the bank of elevators.

"We made it just in time," Zoe whispered.

"I saw him, too. I think it's safe to leave."

"I agree. We need to hurry," Zoe said. Once they had exited the building and were back on the street, she looked at Tina and grinned. "Damn, we're good. I now have a good idea now of how the curse was placed on Ansel."

～◡ル

Whitmire Mansion, Houston, 1939

"Mother, will you stop it. I'm tired of your constant questioning about Ansel's murder." Maxim Delaney swallowed a slug of scotch and rose for a refill. "Would you like another sherry, Mother?"

"Yes, dear, that would be fine." Lucy Whitmire offered the small crystal stem to her son. "Thank you for coming over this evening. I get so lonely these days."

On his way to the bar, Maxim stopped at her words and looked back at his mother. "Lonely? How can you be lonely? People are around here all the time."

"Yes, of course, you're right." Lucy sighed and

twisted her wedding rings. "I know you don't like to hear it, but I'm still not over Ansel's death."

Maxim momentarily paused while pouring his scotch. He added sherry to his mother's glass and returned to the sitting area warmed by the fireplace.

"Mother, I realize you're upset that Ansel's death hasn't been solved. But life goes on. It's been over a year. You need to get back to your normal routine." Maxim's exasperation with his mother's constant discussion of Ansel's death wasn't reflected in his tone. He patted Lucy's hand. "You haven't been to the garden club for months. Isn't there a luncheon next week?"

"Oh, no, dear. I'm simply too upset to resume my social schedule. I won't rest until your brother's killer is arrested." Tears slowly rolled down Lucy's plump cheeks. "Surely, you can understand my pain. He was your only brother."

"How can I forget?"

"Don't be flippant, Maxim." She patted her sunken cheeks with a linen handkerchief. "I must learn who killed Ansel. My life will never be content until I do."

Maxim stood quickly, anger flushing his face. Even in death, Ansel was the center of his mother's life. Damn him to hell! He strode to the doorway and glared at Lucy. "If you're so damn interested in who killed Ansel, why don't you talk to your damned husband."

Chapter Fifteen

After leaving the parking garage a couple blocks from the library, Zoe headed for her parents' house. She and Aunt Tina were meeting Teddy there for dinner and planned to review their trip to the library. She also wanted to see how her father was doing. His trip to the hospital had been a reminder that her parents weren't getting any younger, and she needed to spend more time with them. Quality time, not bringing her troubles to them.

She parked in the driveway behind her mother's white four-door luxury boat of a car. She was determined to make the trip to the library sound like a game and nothing serious. She did not want to visit her childhood home with problems for her parents to solve.

"Mom, Dad, we're here." Zoe and Tina entered through the front foyer and headed toward the family room and kitchen. She heard her mother shout, "Come on back, we're cooking."

David lounged in front of the wide-screen television while Toni stirred a pot on the stove.

Zoe kissed her father and her mother. "What's cooking, Mom?"

"A little this and a little that."

"Toni, you're so descriptive," Tina said while joining her sister at the stove and bumping her at the hip. "Move over and let the master work."

Zoe took that as her cue to leave the kitchen. She moved over to the couch in the family room, close to her father in his favorite leather recliner.

"Hey, Dad." She gazed at her father's eyes, searching for distress, and saw nothing other than her own reflection. "How are you doing? You're looking damn good, by the way."

David reached over and patted his daughter's hand. "Thanks, sweetie, I feel damn good, too." He grinned, squeezed her hand. "Don't worry, I'll be fine. This episode was a reminder I need to take better care of myself—in my old age, that is." His eyes glistened. "Now, tell me what you've been up to."

"It seems so trivial compared to your situation."

"Now, kiddo, don't you go soft on me," David said. "Come on. I can feel it—you've been up to something."

"I'll come clean. Since my offer for Merlin's wasn't accepted, I don't know if I'm out a job or not, but I figure I need to make other plans."

David nodded. "Good thinking."

"I've spent the last two days working on—" The doorbell rang. "I'll get it."

Zoe opened the front door to a smiling male face and ushered him into the house.

"Aunt Tina," she yelled down the hallway, "Teddy's here." She pointed toward the kitchen, "Go straight that way. We can talk later."

Zoe rejoined her father in the family room.

"I need your opinion on something." He nodded, and she continued while twisting her hands in her lap. "Even though the deal with Merlin's fell through, I still want to own a bookstore. I thought I might open a new store focusing on my favorite things."

He raised his eyebrows. "Favorite things?"

"It's a natural for me," she said, hoping he would understand her new great idea. "Books on cooking, wine, and entertaining."

He was silent and Zoe fidgeted. After an eternity he spoke.

"I agree. It's a perfect concept for you. Have you thought of a name for your store?"

"Nope." Zoe blew out a soft breath. "Gourmet Stuff might be cute. My major concern is the money. Do you think the bank loan and the other funds I have will be enough to open a new store?"

"Sweetheart, you'll need twice that amount for a new store. The costs are much more extensive."

Zoe's heart thudded to the floor along with her new idea to secure her future. Damn it. Well, she wouldn't give up. She'd figure out a way to make it happen. Maybe Ansel could help her.

After a glass of pinot noir and a good helping of her mother's lasagna, Zoe loitered at the end of the meal while enjoying the gut feeling of family. Teddy fit into the group as though he had been attending their family dinners for years.

Toni poured mugs of coffee while Tina served homemade chocolate pie.

"If now's a good time, I'd like to hear about your trip to the library today." Teddy glanced around the table before finally settling on Tina's smiling face. "Did anything exciting happen?"

"Other than hiding from the security guard—" Tina winked at him. "It was uneventful."

"What?" Toni asked, concern filling her face.

"Mom, it was nothing. We just made ourselves scarce when he did his rounds," Zoe explained.

"What did you learn?" David questioned.

"Yes, sweetie." Toni's head bounced in the direction of her daughter. "Tell us how you plan to help that poor man stuck in your attic."

Zoe looked around the table at the three people she loved most in the world. Her heart was full and no longer encased in ice. It had been a long time since she'd been this content, even though her job was in severe jeopardy.

"Aunt Tina and I haven't discussed what we each discovered, so this is new information." Zoe looked at her aunt. "I'll go first, okay?"

Tina nodded and sipped her coffee.

Zoe flipped through a couple pages in the notebook she had earlier taken from her purse. "I couldn't find one single entry in Lucy Whitmire's diaries that spelled out the complete description of the curse she placed on her son. Several pages were missing, so I pieced it together myself."

"This sounds interesting," Teddy commented.

Zoe grinned. "I think so. Anyway, I looked at Lucy's diaries for the first five years after Ansel's death. She was incredibly angry he died, to the point of blaming him for causing his own death. She decided he'd been running with the wrong crowd and got mixed up in something bad."

David waved a fork in the air. "Isn't that an unusual attitude for a mother?"

"Seems that way to me, especially when the dead child was the mother's favorite."

"My word," Toni interjected, "the woman must have been nuts."

"You may be right, Mom. She might have been a witch as well. Casting spells was a hobby of hers. The curse she placed on Ansel involved Irish stones. I bought some in New Orleans and discovered they have been used for centuries to place a curse. My guess, interpreting the diary, is that it relates to him staying in the place where he died until the stone is overturned and righted again."

"What in the world does that mean?" Toni looked puzzled.

"Does the curse have a time element with it?" David asked.

Teddy followed with another question. "What happens to Ansel if the curse is broken?"

"I don't think there's any deadline for it to be lifted. I figure Ansel will finally go to his grave when it's resolved. I'm not a hundred percent sure." Zoe pictured him in the rocking chair, casually gracing her attic. Yes, she'd miss him, a lot.

"It makes sense," Teddy added. "We can't forget that Ansel was Lucy's favorite son. She may have been an unusual mother by our standards, but she did love him. His spirit finally connecting with his grave makes perfect sense."

Aunt Tina threw an adoring gaze at Teddy. She

was far beyond smitten. Wedding bells could very well be in the future. Zoe's daydreaming was interrupted by her aunt.

"If that's everything on the curse, let me tell you what I found." Aunt Tina grinned wickedly. "My assignment was to review the family histories. I searched for specific references to Ansel's murder."

"You sound so professional," Toni teased.

"Whatever." Tina ignored her sister's comment and continued with her story. "I discovered that over the seventy years since Ansel's death, there has been much gossip among the family that one of their own was responsible for his murder."

"As in hiring someone to do it?" Zoe asked. She figured if someone Ansel knew had pulled the trigger of the rifle, he would have told her.

"Exactly. I bet a contract killer was hired," Tina said.

Teddy scratched the day's stubble on his chin. "If I remember correctly, William Whitmire, Maxim, and Lucy were the immediate family alive in 1938."

"Yes, but we can't forget the families of Lucy and Ansel Senior's brothers and sisters." Zoe reminded him, "The Dodd family too."

"That's right. Didn't Sara Ford tell us that her grandmother, Suzanne Dodd, and Lucy were best friends for decades?" Tina looked at Zoe for confirmation.

"I read several passages in Lucy's diaries mentioning Suzanne. But seriously, I don't think she should be on our list of suspects." Zoe finished her last bite of pie. "I say we go with Maxim or William

Whitmire. Either of them had the most to gain with Ansel dead."

David chuckled. "Are we voting on this or something?"

"Cute, Dad, real cute," Zoe sputtered.

〰

Zoe was about to put her key in the lock of her front door when the door swung open. Ansel stood in the middle of the living room, glaring as best he could, being a ghost and all.

"Where in the world have you been?"

She shut the door behind her and stared at him. "Remember? The library?"

Their conversation on the subject earlier that morning must have dawned on him because he sheepishly grinned.

"I do remember now. But, we have a problem."

"What now?"

"Your house was broken into again," Ansel stated matter-of-factly.

Zoe glanced around the living room. Nothing seemed out of order. "Are you sure? I don't see a mess."

"They went directly to the attic."

"You saw the burglar?" Zoe asked, her eyes wide in disbelief.

"I know who it was."

"Who?"

Ansel hesitated. His mouth opened and closed, and then he blurted out, "Your friend, Sam."

"Sam? You've got to be kidding."

"I would never joke about something as serious as

this."

"How do you know it was Sam? And why would he break into my house? All he had to do was call me." Zoe didn't want to believe Sam had broken into her home.

"I recognized him from having dinner here a week ago. He and his friend went straight to the attic."

"Friend? He broke into my house with a friend?" She stamped her foot on the floor, daggers firing from her eyes.

"Zoe, please, calm down." Ansel moved to the couch. "Let's sit down. I'll tell you everything from the beginning." He started to sit but then jumped up and moved toward the kitchen. "But first, I'll get you a glass of wine."

Zoe's mind was once again reeling with confusion. Why in the hell would Sam Dodd break into her house and make a beeline for the attic. The attic was empty except for Ansel's presence, his rocking chair, a few boxes of whatever, and the trunk full of books from Merlin's—nothing much of interest, except for Ansel, of course.

He handed her a wineglass. "Enjoy the bouquet."

"I can't get over you being able to hold objects. It's wild." Zoe tasted the wine. "Excellent choice, by the way. Now, tell me about this latest break-in."

"They came in about four hours ago. I assume they had a key—"

"Hold on. Describe the person with Sam?"

"A young woman, maybe twenty-five years old, tall, brown hair. She was comfortable with him, so I assume they knew each other well."

"Like brother and sister? She sounds like Jill, Sam's little sister. She works part-time at Merlin's." Zoe sat on the sofa and put the wineglass between her legs. She rubbed her eyes with both hands. "I can't believe this happened, Sam and Jill breaking into my attic." She looked at Ansel, searching for an answer to her question. "Why? Why in the hell would they do this?"

"I don't know. All I can tell you is that once they got into the attic, they went directly to that old trunk in the corner." Ansel sat in the recliner. "They pulled out every book in it, examined each one. Then Sam yelled a bit before they left. That's it. They left through the front door."

Zoe sipped the wine and analyzed Ansel's words. It sure sounded like they were looking for something in particular. Apparently a book, since that's all that was in the trunk. But what book and why?

"I need to talk to Sam," Zoe said.

"Why in the world would you talk to him?"

"Ansel, think about it. He doesn't know I know he broke into my house." Zoe pursed her lips. "I can catch him off guard."

"Yes, I see your point." He rose and paced the room. "You need to have him relaxed and unaware of your motive for seeing him."

"You want me to drug him?"

"No, of course not. But a nice meal and a glass of vino might do the trick. Once he's relaxed, you can confront him."

Zoe jumped up. "That's a great idea." She approached Ansel with her arms outstretched and then realized she couldn't hug him. "Oh, I love you. You always have the best ideas."

Zoe moved back to the couch, so she missed the shocked expression on his face. He started to speak but quickly recovered and masked his face.

"I'll invite Sam to dinner for tomorrow night. Right, that'll work." Zoe was silent for a moment. "Once he's full and relaxed, I'll pounce on him. I'll call him right now."

∾

An hour later, Ansel found himself at his favorite roost, slowly rocking while spying on the street in front of Zoe's house. He liked her house. No, he loved it. The front reminded him of a gingerbread dollhouse from a child's book. That thought reminded him of Charlotte, who had loved every square inch of the house. She'd be pleased at Zoe's changes, especially the kitchen, with its modern appliances.

Ansel closed his eyes, enjoying the leisurely pace of his rocking, so relaxing, calming. His thoughts softened, and he imagined Zoe spending time with him, but a different kind. Wouldn't that be a hoot? He chuckled and easily pictured the two of them walking hand in hand into a hotel bar, perhaps on the Champs-Élysées in Paris. He escorted her to the table by the window with the best view of the avenue and the Arc de Triomphe. Only the best champagne was poured into Waterford flutes.

They tapped their glasses, and Ansel made a heartfelt toast. "You're my best friend and the keeper of my secrets. Here's to lifelong love and kisses sealed with good wine." Zoe laughed and declared champagne to be her favorite food group. He loved her sense of humor and her ability to adapt to new situations—an excellent example, his transition from ghost to human.

Ah, yes, Zoe was one hell of a woman. Damn, he loved her like, well, like the devil.

After the champagne and a bowl of strawberries and cream, they looked in each other's eyes, and rose in unison from the table. Ansel took her hand in his and brushed his thumb over the top. Her skin was soft and cool. Ah, he loved this woman.

A few minutes later they entered their hotel room, intending to take a nap before a tour of Notre Dame Cathedral. Zoe had a better idea, though, and they never did take that nap.

～⌒

Zoe woke Sunday morning full of plans for the day—first up, a quick trip to the grocery store to purchase the perfect ingredients for the perfect dinner to trap Sam. She knew her plan was perfect. Food was always, next to sex, the best method for a woman to get what she wanted from a man. Since sex wasn't an option, a good meal was the key. She had settled on a simple, yet elegant, menu—broiled salmon, asparagus, and salad. Sam would love it and be putty in her hands.

After returning from the store and preparing her special blue cheese dressing, Zoe climbed the stairs to the study for some quality work on the magazine article. Completing it had been dragging on far too long. She needed to finish it by the end of the week. Experience had taught her to complete an article within a couple of weeks of its beginning. Otherwise, it schlepped on and on.

"This article is good. I like the theme." Zoe scratched her head. "How should it end?"

"How about happily ever after?"

"That would be perfect." Zoe turned to find Ansel in the customary wicker chair. "Other than the fact that perfect anything is totally unattainable. That's unrealistic, by the way."

"You have such a skewed view. Try being more positive."

She laughed. "A spirit attached to my attic for seventy-some years is coaching me to be more positive. Priceless."

"Maybe so, but you do tend to look at the world from a negative stance."

"I call it realistic. I'm not one to sugarcoat the truth."

"Speaking of truth, I have a question for you." Zoe nodded, so Ansel continued. "Last night when I suggested you have Sam to dinner, you said you loved me. What did you mean by that?"

My heavens, what did she mean by that? Was it simply a figure of speech, or did she mean what she said? Yes, she did. But loving Ansel was useless. The love for a ghost wouldn't help her get on with her life, post-Bill and now Sam.

"Zoe, why is loving me hindering your life?"

"Damn it. Stop reading my mind."

"I told you before, it comes with the territory." Ansel pushed his hair back. "Please answer my question."

"Loving you isn't hindering me. It's just useless, a

waste of time. Nothing will ever come of it. Soon you'll be vanished to your grave."

He glanced beyond Zoe's shoulders, then back at her face. "Is that what you truly want, me planted in my grave?"

"Of course not," Zoe cried. "I'd prefer that you were a living, breathing human who could hug me and kiss me, make love to me." She took a deep breath and whispered, "I do love you."

A boom thundered throughout the study, shaking the walls and bouncing the furniture on the floor. Zoe's chair tipped over, spilling her to the carpet. She remained still for a few seconds. She'd never heard of an earthquake hitting Houston. Another boom rippled through her house. She put her hands over her ears and squeezed her eyes shut, praying her house could withstand the aftershocks.

Something touched her shoulder.

"Zoe, are you all right?"

She opened her eyes and looked up from the floor. Ansel stood peering down at her with concerned blue eyes. He reached out to her. "Here, take my hand. Come up slowly."

Zoe took his hand and rose. The warmth and strength of his hand was comforting. It had been awhile since she'd felt that way from simply holding a man's hand.

A man's hand. Holy shit.

Zoe stepped back, looked him up and down. She walked a circle around him and surveyed every inch. He stood quietly and sported a grin.

"Okay, Mr. Delaney, what's up? I just went

through what felt like an earthquake, and you now appear amazingly human." She poked his arm with a finger and felt firm flesh.

She needed to sit down, so she righted the desk chair and slumped in it. "Please, tell me what the hell is going on."

Ansel grinned, similar to exploding fireworks on the Fourth of July. "Actually, you're a genius."

"Please, no games, just tell me the truth."

"The truth, as you say, is that you solved the curse."

Zoe jumped out of her chair. "Solved the curse? No way, I don't know how to. I hadn't figured it out yet."

"You did it by being yourself." Ansel kissed her on the cheek. "Solving the curse canceled my murder."

"You're talking in riddles." She started toward the door of the study. "Let's go to the kitchen, and I'll make another pot of coffee." She muttered under her breath, "I'm sure this human thing is temporary anyway."

Zoe heard Ansel's footsteps as he followed her to the kitchen. He sat at the table while she made the coffee. Neither said a word while the coffee perked. Zoe stared out the window, lost in her own thoughts. How could this be happening? Dead people, ghosts, goblins, didn't turn back into human beings. She glanced at Ansel, who looked human and healthy, much too healthy. Maybe he was now some type of zombie.

Five minutes later, the pot's dripping had ended. Zoe poured and then set two mugs of Gold Coast

Blend on the table. She sat across from Ansel. She sipped the coffee and watched his face while he kept a watch on her.

"All right, enough of this. Please, enlighten me with what's going on. Are you permanently a flesh-and-blood human?"

"First things first," Ansel said with some glee. "Thank you, from the bottom of my heart, for breaking the curse. Even after seventy years, it's still hard for me to believe my own mother placed it on me after my funeral."

"I already told you, Ansel, I don't know the curse's resolution. There's no way on earth I could have broken it. I've just now figured out how it was placed. Let me show you." Zoe went to her purse on the hall table. She'd been keeping the wishing stones in it for safekeeping. She handed the small bag to Ansel.

"What is this?"

"These are Irish wishing stones. I believe your mother used something like these to place the curse on you."

"I see," he said. He poured the stones into his hand, bounced them up and down, his face unreadable. "I do believe you are correct."

"Good. But I still don't know how to resolve the curse."

"Zoe, sweetheart, it's simple. You broke it by saying you loved me, even though that creates an impossible situation in your life."

"Well, duh, being in love with a ghost is a definite buzz kill."

"What in the world does that mean?"

"It means it's an impossible situation. The quicker you're out of my attic, the quicker I can get on with my life and you can get on with yours, whatever that entails." She nodded with satisfaction. "The quicker, the better."

Ansel closed his eyes, opened his eyes, and glanced at the ceiling. He opened his mouth, closed it. He rose and paced the small kitchen, the soles of his leather boots slapping on the tile. "Okay, this is the truth. I am human again. To lift my mother's curse, a human female had to fall in love with me without knowing that was the solution. You came along and—"

"This is not some damned Hollywood movie," Zoe yelled, waving a fist at him. "Things like that don't happen in real life."

"Yet, here we are."

"Here we are indeed." She had to get to the bottom of this. "What about the future? Are you truly human? I've noticed you haven't tasted the coffee yet."

"Yes, I'm the whole enchilada, as I heard in a TV commercial. I'm a tiny bit nervous when it comes to food." He picked up the mug and smelled the edge. He blinked, put the mug to his lips. "Goodness, that's strong coffee."

"That's the best kind. How does your stomach feel?" He shrugged. Zoe looked at her watch. Twelve fifteen. She had a great idea. "Let's try some wine."

He looked doubtful, but said, "Okay. I need to get my stomach back to normal as quickly as I can."

Zoe rose and opened the refrigerator, pulling out cheese and red grapes. She gathered a serving tray, wineglasses, and water crackers. At the same time, Ansel retrieved a bottle of pinot noir from the cooler, along with a corkscrew.

Zoe watched him uncork the wine with the ease of a master. That was it. That was her answer. That was the moment she believed in his rebirth. She felt like giggling and dancing around the kitchen. Instead, she fluffed her hair and wished she had put on lipstick and mascara.

They regrouped at the bistro table. Zoe served the cheese and crackers while Ansel poured two glasses of wine.

"Ansel, I do love you, even though this is totally nuts." Zoe tapped her glass against his. "I don't know what any of this means for me, but I'm thrilled you are now alive and not headed to your grave. How do you feel about . . . uh, the new you?"

"I'll need some time to acclimate to being human again. But let's be honest, I'm thirty-three years old and I don't have a job. I love you with all my heart, but what do I have to offer you? Tales from the crypt to help with your magazine article?"

"Don't worry about that right now. Drink your wine." She raised her glass. "Here's to working on one problem at a time. The current problem is my dinner with Sam this evening. Help me with a kick-ass plan to blindside Sam. We'll discuss this human thing after that."

But wait, Ansel just said he loved her with all his heart. Holy shit.

Chapter Sixteen

Zoe checked her watch for the fifth time in twenty minutes. She had expected Ansel to join her in the kitchen to help. Why had she expected his help? He was raised in a time where women were subordinate to men. A woman seventy years ago would certainly not expect a man to help in the kitchen. Says who?

"Ansel, come on down here," she yelled and shortly heard clomping on the stairs.

Ansel's handsome face soon smiled at her. "Yes, ma'am, at your service."

"Keep me company while I chop the vegetables."

"My pleasure. I have something to tell you." He sat on the stool to the right of the sink. "I've been thinking. Before I can get on with my life, there are a couple of issues I—"

The doorbell rang.

Zoe set the knife on the cutting board and wiped her hands on a dish towel. "Sam must be a few minutes early, so scoot back upstairs."

"Don't I get any dinner?" Ansel asked innocently.

"You can eat after he leaves. I'm sure he won't be here late."

"Whatever." Ansel stomped back up the stairs

while Zoe went to answer the door.

Sam stood on the front porch carrying a bouquet of flowers and wearing a smile.

"Hi Sam, come on in. Dinner's almost ready."

Sam kissed Zoe lightly on the lips and handed her the flowers. "Thanks for asking me over. I missed not seeing you the other night."

"Me, too." She led him to the kitchen and pointed to a pitcher of iced tea and a plate of brie and crackers on the counter. "Help yourself while I put these flowers in water."

She watched Sam out of the corner of her eye. She and Ansel hadn't agreed on the best way to approach him. Whatever. Winging it hadn't gone out of style.

She grabbed a vase from under the sink and plopped in the flowers. After filling it under the faucet, she placed it in the middle of the bistro table, already set for their meal.

"The cheese is excellent," Sam said.

"Good, I tried a new variety." Zoe poured a glass of tea for herself, faced Sam. "How are you? It seems like ages since I've seen you."

"I'm good, working my ass off. How about you?"

Zoe stirred a lemon sauce on the stove. "I'm in limbo right now. My offer to buy Merlin's was turned down, followed by the store being broken into. Mr. Allen isn't too happy with me. I may be out of a job." She drained the asparagus, placed it in a beautiful Italian serving dish, and spooned over the sauce. "Have a seat. Dinner is ready."

She busied herself serving the meal while Sam gathered their glasses and the pitcher of tea. She'd hoped Sam would react to the possibility of her losing her job. That would at least redeem him to a degree. He said nothing.

After a few minutes, Zoe was eager to put her plan into motion.

"Did I tell you my house was broken into yesterday afternoon?" she asked between bites of salad.

"No. Was anything taken?"

"Nothing. The weird thing is that the only place searched was the attic and that old trunk of books from Merlin's."

Zoe watched Sam's face for a sign of anything— admission of the break-in would have been good. He blandly looked at her.

"Was anyone hurt?" he asked.

She noticed he was doing his best to appear nonchalant. She replied, "No, they were dignified burglars."

"You think they were looking for a book?" Sam asked.

"That's what the eyewitness said."

He choked, spitting a piece of salmon onto the table. Zoe jumped from her chair and pounded on his back.

"Are you okay?" She twisted around to look in his face. "Did the meal upset you?"

Sam's eyes watered. "No, no, the dinner is great. I swallowed wrong." He slugged down tea.

She returned to her chair. Enough dangling. "What book were you looking for, Sam?"

"A first edition of *The Adventures of Tom*

Sawyer—" He stopped midsentence. Several moments passed before he spoke again. "You know it was me?"

"And Jill." Zoe allowed that piece of information to soak in. "Why did you think the book was here?"

"It was a last resort." He seemed resigned to having been caught.

"Why didn't you just ask me?"

"It's complicated."

"Come on, Sam, what's the real story?"

He pushed his plate away and carefully set the tea glass on a napkin. After a moment, he spoke. "This began with my father, John Dodd. He grew up in a well-to-do family here in Houston with a love for books. Jack Allen was his best friend since age five."

"You mean the Mr. Allen who owns Merlin's?"

"That's the one," he said. "Once my father got out of college and had his first job, he wanted to make a grand gesture to his childhood friend. He found a first edition of *The Adventures of Tom Sawyer* through a dealer. He gave it to Jack Allen as a gift for his twenty-fifth birthday. The story is that Jack returned it to my father as a wedding gift, eight years later."

"I've never heard Mr. Allen speak about the book."

Sam starred at Zoe. "My guess is that he didn't return it. We haven't found it in any of my father's belongings. He died a couple of years ago." He shrugged. "Jill and I have been looking for it since."

"Why not talk to Mr. Allen?" she suggested. "He's a nice man."

"He and my father had a falling out when my father married. I doubt Jack would be willing to speak to me or Jill if he knew we were John Dodd's kids."

"I think you should. I remember Mr. Allen talking about an old friend of his who had donated a rare first edition to Rice University. Ten to one that rare edition was *Tom Sawyer,* and your father was the donor."

Sam rose and began to pace the kitchen. "Damn it. I never even considered Jack wouldn't have the book." He stopped and stared at Zoe. "I've acted like a fool."

"I won't argue with that. And you broke into my house, twice."

"I'm sorry about that. I can pay for any damage."

"I appreciate that since you've been such a jerk. I'll get a list together for you." Zoe rose, done with Sam, and began to clear the dishes. "Would you like coffee before you leave?"

"No, thanks. I hate to eat and run, but I need to head out. I've got a lot of thinking to do, and I need to talk with Jill."

"I understand." Zoe led him to the front door and waved as he stepped off the porch.

Bet that's the last I hear from him, she thought. No way would he have the nerve to face her again.

❧

"I'm telling you, the guy's a complete moron." Ansel leaned against the kitchen counter watching Zoe rinse off dishes in the sink and load them in the dishwasher. "What intelligent person wouldn't consider the possibility that Jack Allen didn't have the book?"

He'd been ranting about Sam for the past ten minutes. Zoe read between the lines. She could have been hurt during the first break-in, and it would have been Sam's fault. But enough was enough. She was tired of Sam and hearing about his shortcomings.

"May I change the subject, please?"

"I'm sorry. I got a little carried away." Ansel crossed his arms over his chest. "What is the subject now?"

"It seems to me we need to establish some ground rules with you living in my house."

"Ground rules?" He stared at her for a moment, grinned. "I agree one hundred percent. What's your first rule?"

She dried her hands and tossed the dish towel on the counter. "I think we each need to respect the other's privacy. You can sleep in the guest room."

He raised his eyebrows.

"You'll be comfortable there. We, uh, both expressed some feelings about the other." Zoe picked up the dish towel and folded it. "The situation is different now, and we shouldn't be held to what either of us said in a moment of stress. I mean, we've never even been on a date together."

"Date?"

"Oh, for God's sakes, a date is when the man takes the woman out to dinner and opens doors for her." Zoe slapped the towel on the counter and headed out of the kitchen.

"Zoe, wait, please." He grabbed her hand and rubbed his thumb over the palm. "You know there's a tremendous amount I have to learn about modern life."

"Didn't you pay attention at all, watching thousands of hours of television over the years?"

"Sometimes," he shrugged. "Mostly, it was

entertainment."

"That's it. I need a break from you right now. See you in the morning." She pulled her hand from his and marched toward the hall and up the stairs to her bedroom. The walls vibrated at the slam of the door.

Zoe flung herself into the middle of the bed, grabbing a pillow and hugging it to her chest.

She muttered into the pillow, "I fell in love with a damn ghost who turned into a damn man who doesn't know what a damn date is. Urrghh." Her fists beat the pillow while tears trailed down her cheeks. She glared at the ceiling. "Why does all this crap happen to me?"

∿

Relaxing on a bed was wonderful. Ansel crossed his arms behind his head and surveyed the room. Yellow and purple-flowered curtains on the window matched the bedspread beneath him. The room was prim and neat and so unlike Zoe.

Ah, Zoe, his savior and his biggest headache. Somehow he had to convince her they had a future together. Marriage was what he intended. Assuming he could support her as any good husband should. No wife of his was going to work unless it was for fun. He chuckled. That had the potential for an interesting conversation.

She was an independent woman and wouldn't take kindly to his trying to manage her. That meant, of course, he would have to be especially crafty in convincing her that doing what he wanted was really her idea, including marriage. He was up to the challenge. After all, she had called him a charmer more than once.

His thoughts turned to the next morning. He fully expected to have his first major argument with Zoe. It was unavoidable. His plans did not include her, and she would be unhappy about it, probably furious. She'd say it was ridiculous that she couldn't tag along with him. He could live with her anger.

The one bonus of a major argument with a woman was, well . . . makeup sex. An idea he could wrap his mind around. He closed his eyes and thought back to the first time he had seen Zoe after she had inherited her Nana's house. He'd been very unhappy at being stuck in a cold house all by himself since the owner had died a month before. The house had been deserted other than one visit from her family to clean out all her belongings. Thank heavens they forgot to check the attic and didn't grab the rocking chair.

He heard a car door slam and looked out the front window, figuring the teenagers next door were at it again. They played the loudest and worst music imaginable while washing their cars—a strange custom. He peered through a slit in the blinds, and no teenagers were out. It was the granddaughter, Zoe. She hadn't been back to the house since Nana had passed on.

She struggled to open the front door, or so he guessed based on the noise, but then finally the lock clicked and something thumped against the wood. The door slowly swung open. Ansel raced back to his perch on the stairs.

Zoe stood in the doorway, framed by the morning sun streaming in behind her. Her arms were loaded with large paper bags, a broom, and a black box of some sort. She struggled through the living room and then collapsed on the yellowed linoleum in the middle of the kitchen. Contents of the bags skidded to every corner, and the broom landed under her knees.

The wind must have been knocked out of her. She was silent for several moments. Ansel squinted for a clearer view of her face. He was certain she was going to cry, a typical feminine reaction.

Her reaction surprised him, and he wondered how she knew so many swear words—that's when his crush on Zoe grew its wings.

∿

Monday dawned with the promise of sunshine and a warm afternoon. Zoe hadn't slept well and failed to notice the day around her while getting the newspaper from the front walk. Ansel sat at the table when she reentered the kitchen.

"Good morning. I poured coffee." He smiled and motioned toward the counter. "The pot had stopped making noise."

"Thanks." Zoe tossed the paper on the table. She was determined to maintain a positive attitude in front of Ansel. "Would you like breakfast? Eggs, cereal, or a muffin?"

"Hmm, eggs. Do you have any bacon?"

"Sure. I'll fix you some. Check out the paper. You might enjoy the latest news."

For the next several minutes, Zoe sipped coffee and busied herself with creating a quick breakfast for her guest. That's how she was referring to Ansel in her mind—a guest who would soon leave and go on to his own life.

The breakfast disappeared in record time.

"Your eggs are delicious." Ansel scooped the last bite off his plate.

"Thanks." Zoe felt much better after food and coffee. "I add cream cheese and chives and a tiny pinch of red pepper."

"I like this modern way of cooking." Ansel leaned over and kissed Zoe full on the lips.

Her initial surprise at the gesture quickly morphed to concern. "Hey, none of that. No kissing. Remember, you're concentrating on you first, not me and you."

"You're right. But I do need your help. I need to call a taxi to take me to the J&L offices, and I need to borrow money from you to pay for it."

"You don't need a taxi. I'm going with you, and I'll drive."

"No, you're not. I'm doing this on my own," Ansel said sternly. "I'm fully capable of—"

"Are you freaking nuts? You don't even know the people at J&L."

"As I was saying, I'm fully capable of having an intelligent and dignified conversation with Robert Delaney, my, uh, nephew," Ansel said with the confidence of a former ghost.

"Have you considered that he'll think you're a fake or a charlatan?" Zoe knew she had to protect him.

"Was there a drama pill in your eggs?" Ansel asked with rolling eyes.

"Damn it, Ansel, be serious." Zoe stomped a foot. "You need my help to navigate through modern life. What about everything you don't know about? Like, say a margarita or a laptop computer."

"Do you think I'm stupid?" Ansel asked while puffing out his chest. "I've spent the last fifty years watching television, first with your grandmother and recently with you. It's a darn good eye on the world. I know about presidential politics, the price of a gallon of gas, and global warming."

"I thought you said your TV watching was mostly entertainment. Besides, you don't know Houston."

"I'm going alone. Again, may I borrow some money? I'll pay you back."

"This is ridiculous. I'll call a cab."

"I already did," Ansel said. "It should be here in a couple of minutes."

"Fine, wait here." Zoe marched upstairs for her wallet. She returned with cash and a piece of paper and handed both to Ansel. "There should be enough money for two taxi rides and lunch downtown. The paper has my address, and my home and cell numbers." She grinned slowly, "Just in case you get lost."

"Excellent. Thank you."

Zoe didn't like Ansel's tone, but he was a big boy, and if he wanted to do this on his own, then fine.

The taxi honked in the drive way.

Ansel studied Zoe. "I know you're not happy with me right now. All I ask is that you give me a chance to prove myself."

"You better get going," she replied.

Zoe studied Ansel as he walked toward the taxi. Who would imagine that twenty-four hours ago he had been a simple spirit stuck between life and death in her attic? He now looked young and energetic and stubborn as hell.

He climbed into the backseat of the taxi and it sped down the street.

Zoe wandered through the living room, straightening a picture frame and a magazine, and then went back to the kitchen. She cleared off the dishes, left them soaking in the sink, and poured another cup of coffee. Her mind couldn't escape her last conversation with Ansel.

He didn't understand her. How could he expect her to jump into a romance with him, considering the sad ending to her five years with Bill? Didn't he realize that for a relationship to endure, time and trust and commitment were required?

Zoe knew she couldn't give her heart to him without knowing his would be given as well. And what did she know about Ansel, other than what she'd read in a family history or heard from a family member whom he had never met? Now that she thought about it, he'd told her little about his human life.

A thought crossed her mind, and she went with it. He had used her. Ansel had purposely set out to woo her so she'd eventually cause his mother's curse to break. Poor Ansel, the jerk, he'd had to wait seventy long years until the right unsuspecting female moved into the house. What a fool she had been.

She finished the coffee and added the cup to the sink. He'll be out of the house by evening, and then good riddance. Let the Delaney's take him in. They were rich and could afford another mouth at the dinner table. She remembered her magazine article and the ending as the last piece to write. Talk about the perfect conclusion.

In the study, she pulled up the article's file on her computer. She starred into space for a few moments and then began to furiously pound the keyboard.

Not every good story has a happy ending. In this case, however, it is a most happy and auspicious ending. The spirit has departed the building. Of course, producing this result was not an easy undertaking. It involved a dose of good fortune, meticulous research, and a will to succeed. Indeed, the most difficult part of —

The phone rang.

"Good morning, Zoe. This is Mr. Allen."

Crap, she should have gone to Merlin's this morning. "How was your vacation?"

"Fine, just fine. Now, my dear, I hope you'll come down to the store this morning. The new owner is here, and I'd like for all of us to talk."

"I'm not sure that's such a good idea."

"I understand your misgivings. However, please humor an old man."

Zoe hesitated for a moment, but her respect for Mr. Allen won. "I'll be there in an hour."

Within thirty-five minutes, Zoe backed out of her driveway. She had no desire to meet whoever had ruined her chance at owning Merlin's. Yet, Mr. Allen had been good to her over the past three years and had provided her the opportunity to discover her passion for working in a bookstore. She would do her best to get through the meeting.

Maybe she could get a job at one of the mega

stores. On second thought, that would be like working in a bank, boring and with no future. Perhaps she should get serious about opening her own bookstore. That would be smart.

Zoe entered Merlin's through the front door. A couple of customer's browsed the Halloween books, and several surrounded a new display of cookbooks. Bingo. Everyone loves a good cookbook.

"Hi," Zoe said. Jill worked the front desk. "Where's Mr. Allen?"

Jill nodded toward the office. "He's in the back with the new owner."

"Thanks." Zoe walked around the counter and pushed aside the curtain before entering the office. Mr. Allen sat in the chair while Sam hovered over him. Both of them were studying something on the desk.

"I'm here."

Mr. Allen rose and kissed Zoe on the cheek. "Thank you so much for coming in, my dear."

"No problem." She turned to Sam. "What are you doing here? Where's the new owner?"

Zoe watched Mr. Allen and Sam glance at each other. Sam licked his lips.

Reality dawned on Zoe. She pointed at Sam. "You're the new owner?"

He nodded.

Zoe burst out laughing. Out of the corner of her eye, she noticed Jill standing in the doorway. She laughed even harder.

After several moments she noticed three sets of eyes carefully watching her. Mr. Allen looked truly concerned.

She held up a hand. "Please, let me catch my breath." She took a couple of deep breaths. Finally she said, "Okay, I'm better. You must realize this is a huge surprise to me. I had no idea Sam, and Jill I suppose, were the other bidders."

Jill gently placed a hand on Zoe's arm. "We didn't mean to go around your back, but we had a good reason to own the store."

"I'm guessing to search for *The Adventures of Tom Sawyer*."

"I've already explained to Mr. Allen what we talked about last night," Sam said. "You were right, Zoe. Father did donate the book to Rice University."

"Like I told you last night, Sam, all you had to do was ask."

"You're absolutely correct," he sheepishly agreed. "We do have a question for you, though."

Zoe raised her eyebrows. "What question?" Before Sam could reply, she continued. "I'll tell you what. If you'll answer a question of mine, then I'll answer yours." Her glance moved from Mr. Allen to Sam to Jill. "Fair enough?"

"Of course, my dear, how can we help you?" Mr. Allen said.

"The question is for all three of you. Did John Dodd ever talk about his father, and if he did, what did he say?"

Jill quickly looked at her brother. He slowly nodded, and she spoke. "Dad never knew his father. He died a few months before Dad was born."

"Our grandfather was murdered," Sam added. "The killer was never found."

"Did your family talk about him? Even though he had passed on, I mean."

Jill laughed. "Great-grandmother Delaney was nuts about him. She talked about Ansel to anyone who would listen."

"Yeah, it's too bad he died. He sounded like a cool guy." Sam grinned. "Grandma Charlotte always said great things about him, even though she married his brother. He was a great athlete and a good businessman. Ansel was one of those topics that always received lots of family gossip."

"Yeah, he was the kind of guy I'm looking for. He was good-looking, too. Grandma said that's where we got our good looks." Jill laughed and poked her brother in the side.

Zoe mulled over everything she had just heard. Was it possible that he truly was a good guy and not a jerk? Had she misjudged Ansel? She remembered what he had said last night. *I love you with all my heart, but what do I have to offer you?*

Ta-dah! Everything now made sense. He was trying to protect her from another ruined relationship. *Well, the hell with that.*

"Good luck with the store. I've got to go." Zoe turned to leave. "Call me tomorrow with your question."

Jill shouted to her retreating back. "Where are you going?"

"To find your grandfather."

Chapter Seventeen

Zoe was right. Houston had changed. The taxi zipped down streets and through intersections he had no hope of recognizing. Being a prudent man, Ansel reconciled himself to not knowing his location. He'd buy a street map as soon as possible.

After twenty minutes, the taxi stopped along another street in downtown Houston he didn't know. Ansel paid the driver and exited onto the sidewalk. His eyes traveled upwards and couldn't take in the enormity of the building in front of him. It blocked out the sun. This was the home office of J&L Manufacturing?

He shrugged off his questions and entered through a set of double doors. The marble lobby was enormous and filled with people rushing in all directions. At the center sat a high, circular desk with the word "Information" sitting on the counter. That's where he headed.

"Excuse me," Ansel said to the older gentleman sitting at the desk. "What floor are the executive offices of J&L Manufacturing?"

"Yes, sir, fiftieth floor." The man pointed to his right. "Take the last bank of elevators at the end of the lobby. May I have your name? I'll let them know you're on your way."

"Yes." Ansel grinned and winked. "Tell them Ansel Delaney III is coming home."

He had previously ridden in an elevator many times, but not one with mirrors lining the walls and door. He looked at his reflection and fluffed his hair. Not bad for a hundred-plus-year-old ghost and new human man. Within a few short seconds, the doors opened to another enormous lobby.

The old family business must have hit the mother lode based on the elegance. He noticed the Waterford chandelier in the middle of the reception area. Both his father and his mother would be embarrassed by such an ostentatious show of success. What had happened to this family?

Ansel strode purposefully to the reception desk.

"Good morning, I'm Ansel Delaney. I'd like to speak to Robert Delaney Senior." The receptionist simply gawked at him. "Now, please." After a moment she came to her senses and mumbled something into a phone. She pointed to a sofa near a bank of windows. "Please have a seat. Mr. Delaney will be with you shortly."

He wandered to the windows. The Houston skyline was incredible. The change in the city over the years was astounding. And more staggering was J&L's contribution to the growth. He rubbed his eyes. His father would be so proud to know his company was living and breathing nearly one hundred years after its birth.

The receptionist interrupted his musings.

"Sir, Mr. Delaney is ready for you. Go through those etched doors at the end of the hall."

Ansel walked across the reception area toward a set of massive glass doors. Without realizing it, he had transferred into business mode. Funny how once those brain synapses powered up, they jumped to the diamond level.

He stopped five feet from the door to remind himself this would be a strange meeting, but he could deal with it. Right then, he could deal with anything. Ansel flexed his shoulders and walked through the doors into the presidential suite. The secretary motioned him to a wide oak door to her right. He pushed it open and found his nephew's office. A tall, gray-haired man stood in front of a massive desk.

"Good morning, I'm Ansel Delaney. And, you must be Maxim's son." He offered his hand to Robert, who declined. "I won't shock you if that's what you're worried about."

"I'm afraid I don't understand who you are. I will admit I was curious because of the name."

"Oh, come on, Robert. You know about the infamous curse my mother placed on me. Only it backfired on you. It brought me back to life rather than sending me to my grave."

"You're insane." Robert glared at Ansel.

"Then why aren't you tossing me out of your office?"

Before Robert could answer, both men turned at the sound of a knock on the door.

"Bobby, we have a guest," Robert said.

Bobby sauntered into the office and gave his

great-uncle a thorough once-over.

"So, you're the Delaney who was murdered and came back to life due to the love of a good woman," Bobby said.

Robert studied his son. "Surely you don't believe in this ridiculous story?"

"Of course I do. Granddad Maxim always told me his mother's curses had magical powers."

Ansel looked from father to son. "Anything else Maxim used to tell either of you? Like who set up my murder?"

"This damned conversation is absurd." Robert pointed a finger at Ansel. "You're obviously an impostor who has private information about our family. You can read it at the library down the street."

"Tell me what you know about my murder," Ansel snapped. "I need to know who killed me."

"Uncle Ansel, I don't share my father's misgivings. I figure you're the real deal. No one has ever accused our family of being normal." Bobby moved to the bar and pulled a bottle of vodka off a glass shelf. "Anyone care for a Bloody Mary?"

Robert and Ansel shook their heads.

"Fine." Bobby poured mixer into the liquor and stirred. "My take on this whole murder scenario is that your mother's second husband, William Whitmire, arranged your death."

"Bobby, that's absurd," Robert exclaimed. "You have no proof."

"Au contraire, father dear." Bobby raised his glass in salute. "I have the check that paid the killer. Granddad gave it to me for safekeeping years ago."

Robert's chin fell to his chest.

Ansel again stepped to the window, trying to absorb the revelation. His mother would be haunting the Whitmires if she knew William had arranged his death. That made him chuckle. He'd vowed in the taxi not to react to anything Robert said. At the time, he hadn't known about Bobby. It was harder than he expected. He'd like nothing better than to knock Bobby on his ass. What a pompous jerk. What had the Delaney family evolved into? Zoe would be laughing her head off if she were here.

It was time to lay all the cards out on the table.

Ansel walked back to the center of the office. Bobby sipped his drink while Robert sat at the bar and peered into space.

"I think we need to talk about the company," Ansel said.

"Excuse me, talk about what?" Robert asked. A worried look flashed across his face.

"The company is no business of yours," Bobby chimed in.

"Gentlemen, now that I know who arranged my murder, the only other issue is who's in control of J&L Manufacturing."

"You're insane," Robert declared. "I'm president, and that's not going to change until I'm ready to change it."

"Dad, I'm in charge of this," Bobby declared with a snarl. "You're retiring next month, and I will start taking over the company now."

Ansel went to the bar. "Bobby, I think you need to read the bylaws of the corporation. My father drew them up and had the foresight to consider circumstances such as this. That particular section is written in stone. It can't be altered. Isn't that right, Robert?"

Robert rubbed his eyes with both palms. "He's right. The oldest Delaney has control until he surrenders that control to another Delaney."

Ansel nodded to Robert. "Thank you. I don't think I'll relinquish that control to you, Bobby." He gazed with disgust at this great-nephew and then moved back toward the windows.

Behind Ansel's back, Bobby opened a drawer beneath the counter and pulled out a handgun.

"Bobby, no," Robert cried.

Ansel turned at the sound of Robert's voice and witnessed Bobby holding a gun pointed dead center at his chest.

He noticed the gun rise slightly, and then something smashed into his legs, causing him to fall sideways to the floor. A bullet shattered a window behind him.

"You son of a bitch," Zoe screamed. She scrambled up from the floor and ran after Bobby, who had exited the office and was running toward the outside hall and the elevator.

"Zoe, stop," Ansel shouted. "Help me get up."

She ran back to him and supported his arm while he struggled to stand.

Robert didn't move. His eyes flew from Ansel to the glass on the floor to the door his son had run out of. He stood and addressed Ansel. "Please help him. He didn't mean to shoot you."

"Are you okay?" Zoe searched Ansel's face for any sign of pain. He hadn't been hit.

"I'm fine. But what the hell are you doing here?"

"I'll tell you later." Zoe grabbed Ansel's hand. "Come on, we need to find Bobby."

Ansel shouted over his shoulder to Robert, "Call the police."

"Let's go to the lobby. Maybe he'll try for the garage." Zoe punched the elevator button and turned to Ansel. "Are you sure you're okay?"

He firmly kissed her on the lips. "Perfect, now that you're with me."

"Oh, baby." She blinked her eyes, "You're such a charmer."

The elevator doors opened, and they rushed into the empty box. Within seconds they were on the first floor.

They both scanned the lobby. No sign of Bobby.

"Why don't you check the garage, and I'll go outside," Ansel said. Zoe nodded and ran toward the left side of the lobby.

Ansel headed for the double doors leading to the sidewalk. Once there, he searched for Bobby. No sight of him. While debating whether to go back into the building, he heard shouts and an awful screeching sound followed by a soft thud. Down the block, people were running into the middle of the street. He did the same.

A large work truck idled with the driver standing next to the front grill. Ansel moved closer. A body lay on the pavement, blood already forming a puddle near the head. There was no doubt in his mind. Bobby was dead.

Ansel rubbed his eyes, brushed his hands through his hair. He had a thousand unanswered questions, the first being "why?" No company was worth killing or dying for. He felt an arm on his sleeve.

"Hey," Zoe said. "You're not responsible for this."

"I know," he agreed. Someone laid a jacket over the body. "Do you have your cell phone? We need to call Robert."

～～

An hour later, Ansel, Zoe, and Robert huddled around the bar in Robert's office. Each held a crystal tumbler containing eighteen-year-old scotch.

"Mr. Delaney, I'm so sorry this happened," Zoe said. "If there's anything I can do . . ."

"Thank you. But I owe you an apology." Robert gazed at her with watery eyes. "I wasn't straight with you before."

"That's all in the past now," she said.

"I just want you to know Bobby arranged for that truck to scare you in New Orleans and the burglary of that bookstore. I'm so sorry I didn't try to stop him."

Zoe understood Robert's need to apologize for his mistakes. A similar *I'm sorry* session with Ansel was on her agenda.

"Robert, we need to notify his wife and family." Ansel didn't want anyone close to Bobby to hear about his death over the news.

"Nancy and the twins are in London on a school trip. I'm sure his assistant has their itinerary." Robert rose slowly from the stool. "I'll go find her."

Ansel and Zoe watched Robert shuffle across the

oak floor to the doors of his office. He hesitated, looking right and left.

"Poor man, can't we call someone for him?" Zoe asked.

"I asked his assistant to contact his wife." He patted Zoe's hand. "She should be here any minute."

Zoe studied Ansel's face. It had changed. The sexy charmer had disappeared. In its place was a sexy man at ease with, and in charge of, his environment. Now wasn't the time to point it out to him. But, definitely . . . later.

"Zoe, why don't you go home," Ansel said. "I need to take care of some things here, and it may take a couple of hours."

"I can wait for you."

"No, go on home. I'll get a taxi back to your house."

"I'll leave you to your business." She kissed his cheek. "See you when you get home."

Chapter Eighteen

Saturday afternoon was the ideal time to finish the magazine article. Zoe sandwiched the time between a sexy start to the day with Ansel the hunk and a family dinner that evening.

In the study, she read what she had typed a week ago. Obviously, she hadn't been happy with the ghost back then. She highlighted the unwanted sentences with the mouse, pressed Delete.

Let's try again. The story had a happy ending buried in there somewhere. Oh, yes.

"Zoe, something's bubbling on the stove," Ansel yelled up the stairs.

"The ravioli." Zoe jumped from the chair and ran downstairs to the kitchen. Sure enough, the pot was at a rapid boil. She lowered the heat to a simmer. She planned on deep-frying the ravioli for an appetizer.

She heard Ansel clapping in the living room while watching a football game on the new plasma television. She plopped next to him on the sofa.

"Thanks." She nuzzled his neck. "Whatcha doing?"

"Waiting for you." He kissed the palm of her hand. "Done with the article?"

"Doing the conclusion now."

"Hmm, it's halftime." He grinned and wrapped his arms around her waist. "Let's get busy."

Two hours later the second batch of ravioli finished cooking. The first pot burned due to inattention from the cook. Zoe smiled as she stirred her sauce and remembered the time she had just spent on her couch. It could no longer be labeled a virgin sofa.

Ansel came into the kitchen with wet hair and smelling of soap. He came up behind Zoe and snuggled against her with his arms around her waist.

"I'm ready to work. How can I help you with dinner?"

"Hmm, let me think." Zoe pulled his arms tighter around her. "My marinara sauce is ready. The meatballs have thawed. Why don't you chop some onions and carrots for the salad?"

Ansel kissed her on the neck and moved to the sink. "Gladly, babe." He pulled out several carrots and began to peel them like Zoe had taught him. "The first time we really talked was right here in the kitchen. You were making the same marinara sauce."

"I remember." She smiled at him, her eyes sparkling. "It seemed like the perfect dish, considering this is our first family dinner together."

"Whatever you say, boss. I hope your family approves of me."

"You sound like you're fifteen. Of course they'll like you." She winked. "But don't rattle any chains. I doubt they'll get the joke."

The guests soon arrived, and the conversation was nonstop before and during dinner. Zoe gathered dishes off the dining room table and carried them to the kitchen. Her mother and Aunt Tina followed.

The trio huddled in a corner out of sight of the entrance to the dining room.

"He is so cute, and a gentleman," Aunt Tina said with obvious glee. "Way to go on cracking that old curse."

"Sweetie, is he, uh, staying here with you?" Leave it to Mom to get right to the point.

"Yes," Zoe said, grinning like a yellow daisy facing the sun. "I can assure you his intentions are honorable."

"I'm more interested in the impact on you." Concern was obvious in Toni's eyes.

"Mom, I know what I'm doing, so don't worry. Ansel and I will be just fine. That reminds me, I have good news—"

"Oh, I forgot," Aunt Tina whispered while dragging her left hand in front of Zoe's face. "Look, Teddy and I are engaged."

Zoe was speechless for a moment. She hugged her aunt fiercely. "Congratulations, this is wonderful."

"We've decided to have the ceremony in the Bahamas, so everyone is invited and we'll have a fabulous vacation."

"Count me in," Zoe said. "Mom, get that champagne out of the refrigerator, and I'll get the cheesecake. This calls for a toast and a treat."

A few minutes later they carried the bubbly and the dessert to the dining room. David poured the champagne while Ansel served the cheesecake.

Teddy rose. "I'd like to make the toast if that's

okay." He glanced around the table and continued. "To my darling Tina, who has lit my life like a firecracker. You are my one true love, and I thank god we've found each other again." He raised his glass, as did everyone else at the table. "Here's to a wonderful rest of our lives."

Zoe and Ansel glanced at each other, both grinning their butts off.

Teddy returned to his seat, and Aunt Tina beamed. She looked at Zoe. "Didn't you say you had some news?"

"I do." Zoe glanced at her parents. "I hope you'll all support me in my new business endeavor."

"Before you go into that," David said. "What happened with Mr. Allen and him filing charges against you for that break-in?"

Zoe nodded her head. "Right, I forgot about that. No charges, and Sam is keeping the store."

"But, who broke in?" Tina asked.

"The detective told me it was one of those gang initiations." Zoe and Ansel had earlier decided that telling her family the truth about Bobby's role was unnecessary and safer for everyone. One white lie wouldn't push them into a life of dishonesty.

"Goodness," Toni said. "That is so sad. Why are there gangs?"

"Mom, my news?" Zoe chimed in.

Toni exchanged a look with David. "Sorry, now what did you want to tell us?

"I didn't want to talk to y'all until I spoke with the bank." Zoe grinned, a blush toasting her cheeks. "But, this is the deal. I'm opening a new bookstore—one that focuses on the cookbook market and accessories."

"That's a wonderful idea," David exclaimed.

"Thanks, Dad. I was hoping you'll still provide your financial support."

"Absolutely." David and Toni said in unison.

"Where is it?" Aunt Tina asked. "I hear location is everything."

Zoe laughed. "It's three doors down from Merlin's Favorite Bookstore, next to the ice cream store. Great location, huh?"

Ansel piped up, "And, it has the perfect name for a store focusing on cookbooks."

Everyone looked at Zoe.

"Okay, all right. The name I've chosen is Gourmet Essentials. Do you like it?"

～

It was near midnight on a Saturday evening in late October. The temperature had dropped to an unexpected fifty-five degrees. Cuddle weather.

Zoe hugged the extra pillow on her bed while pounding her heels on the mattress like a three-year-old receiving her first baby doll on Christmas morning. Damn, she was happy. Funny how life had a way of turning out the way it should. Yep, she'd finally crossed a finish line of sorts. She's solved Ansel's curse, admitted aloud to being in love with him, and told her family she was starting a brand new business. Yep, life was good. She would count her blessings each and every day.

The bathroom door opened, and Ansel joined her on the bed. "Hey, babe, miss me?"

"Hmm, not sure." Zoe pulled away from Ansel for

a mere second before flinging herself on his chest. "Guess I did miss you, and I forgot to tell you something."

"What? Like how much you love me?"

"That I do. I discovered the mystery of the white roses on your grave."

"How are they getting there?" He stroked a hand along her upper arm.

"Your mother's estate took care of it. I asked the florist to transfer the flowers to your father's grave. I hope that's okay."

"That's great detective work, Miss Miller. Thank you for thinking about my dad." Ansel sent her the sweetest gaze. "I've been thinking about something."

"Oh, yeah?" Zoe kissed his chest. "But first, I have something to tell you."

"What?"

"It's a family issue . . . mmm, actually more of a situation."

"Why so serious? Issue or situation, tell me."

She hesitated as she had no idea how he'd take this piece of news. "Remember I'm simply the messenger." She pulled away from him and sat on the bed, her hands clasped together. "This is the deal . . . Sam Dodd, and his sister Jill, are your grandchildren."

He threw her a look that could have boiled a chicken. "What are you talking about? That moron Sam is my grandson? How in the hell could that be true?"

"Hold on." She placed a hand on his chest. "Hear me out. Your son with Charlotte, John Dodd, married and had two children—Sam and Jill. Thus, they are your biological grandchildren."

Ansel jumped off the bed and began to pace the bedroom. Zoe stayed quiet, allowing him to process the bombshell she had released. Finally he stopped, threw her a gaze filled with amazement and sat in front of her on the bed. He took her hands and held them gently in his.

"This is one hell of a surprise. I've not given one serious thought to any descendants from my tryst with Charlotte. Silly on my part, but I do have a plan."

"A plan?" Her breath hitched, he hadn't been human long enough to have a decent plan. "That was quick, I can't wait to hear it."

"Actually Robert came up with the idea. Since I'm taking over J&L, we needed a reasonable explanation as to my sudden appearance. We've concocted a story about my father having a step-brother he never knew and long story short, I'm a long-lost Delaney cousin."

She considered his idea, yep, that would work. "This will allow you to get to know Sam and Jill without freaking them out, or you."

"That's what I'm thinking. Also, I have another plan." He kissed the tip of her nose, drew back, and cupped her face in his hands. "I think we should get married."

At first Zoe wasn't sure she had heard him correctly. Marry a man over a hundred years old?

"Don't forget I'm only thirty-three in human years," he reminded her.

Here we go again. Zoe wrapped her arms around his neck and whispered in his ear. "Excellent idea, Mr. Delaney. I accept."

*The greatest thing you'll ever learn is simply to
love and to allow love in return.*

One last thought:

Q: Why didn't the ghost go to the party?

A: Because he had no body to go with.

If you enjoyed this novel, please leave a review on
Amazon, or on Goodreads, if you are a member. Many
thanks!

ZOE'S MARINARA SAUCE

Ingredients
- ½ cup extra-virgin olive oil
- 1 large white onion, finely chopped
- 2 garlic cloves, finely chopped
- 2 stalks celery, finely chopped
- 2 carrots, peeled and finely chopped
- ½ teaspoon sea salt
- ½ teaspoon freshly ground black pepper
- 2 tablespoons chopped fresh parsley leaves
- 2 – 32 ounce cans peeled Italian tomatoes or crushed tomatoes
- 2 dried bay leaves

Directions
- In a large pot, heat the olive oil over medium heat
- Add onions and garlic, sauté until the onions are translucent, 10 minutes or so
- Add carrots, celery, and salt and pepper; sauté until all vegetables are soft
- Add parsley, tomatoes, and bay leaves and mix well
- Simmer uncovered over low heat until the sauce thickens, an hour or so
- Remove the bay leaf from the sauce
- Season to taste with additional salt and pepper
- The yield is 2 quarts sauce
- Serve with your favorite pasta

Zoe likes to add Italian sausage with the garlic and onions—pour the meat sauce over spaghetti with tons of grated Romano-Parmesan cheese. Molto bene!

ABOUT THE AUTHOR

Karen Sue Burns

Karen Sue Burns writes romantic suspense and mystery featuring feisty heroines who find themselves embroiled in risky situations full of adventure and sexy heroes.

Karen has been a writer since 8th grade. Her day job as a CPA has provided interesting experiences: travel to Rio de Janeiro, London, and Oslo, auditing wine bottle glass molds in California, and taking a helicopter to a drillship off the Texas Gulf Coast. Accounting has been good to her, but writing romance and mystery novels is her passion. She enjoys cooking and creating recipes so her heroines do the same. All of her indie anthologies and novels include one of her favorite recipes. *In Hot Pursuit* is her debut romantic suspense novel. She is also a contributor to the sweet and sensual romance anthology series *Seasons of Love* with the books *Hearts, Hearths and Holidays; Spring Promise; and Sweet Summertime Love*. Readers may contact Karen via the Bio/Contact tab on her website. Check out the Recipe tab while you're there!

Find Karen Here:

Website: http://karensueburns.com
Facebook: http://facebook.com/KarenSueBurns
Twitter: http://twitter.com/karensueburns
Blog: http://karensueburns.com/blog
Pinterest: http://pinterest.com/KarenSueBuns